Lynne & Perry

Behind Enemy Lines

I HOPE YOU ENJOY THIS

LOVE + BLESSINGS
+ A BIG HUG!

Mark Dikell
xx

Behind Enemy Lines

Malcolm Rothwell

Copyright © 2019 by Malcolm Rothwell.

ISBN: Softcover   978-1-9845-8901-9
         eBook   978-1-9845-8900-2

All rights reserved. No part of this book may be reproduced or transmitted in any form or by any means, electronic or mechanical, including photocopying, recording, or by any information storage and retrieval system, without permission in writing from the copyright owner.

This is a work of fiction. Names, characters, places and incidents either are the product of the author's imagination or are used fictitiously, and any resemblance to any actual persons, living or dead, events, or locales is entirely coincidental.

Any people depicted in stock imagery provided by Getty Images are models, and such images are being used for illustrative purposes only.
Certain stock imagery © Getty Images.

Print information available on the last page.

Rev. date: 07/23/2019

To order additional copies of this book, contact:
Xlibris
800-056-3182
www.Xlibrispublishing.co.uk
Orders@Xlibrispublishing.co.uk
794111

CONTENTS

Introduction ix

1   Behind Enemy Lines 1
2   In the Beginning 6
3   Finding My Bearings 13
4   North Wales 18
5   Some Answers 23
6   More Training 26
7   Tension Mounts 31
8   Language Difficulties 36
9   Action Stations 39
10   A Romantic Assignment 45
11   Explosive Outcomes 51
12   A Bridge Too Far? 56
13   Afloat 63
14   The Rhine 66
15   Incarceration 69
16   The Unexpected 73
17   Father Rhine 77
18   God Talk 81
19   Alarm Bells 84
20   The Flying Dutchman 88
21   The Black Forest 92
22   The Cave 96
23   The Descent 98
24   Lake Constance 101
25   Endings and a Beginning 104

To three lifelong friends and their lovely wives:
David and Wylan Horsfall
John and Brenda Powney
David and Christine Scarisbrick

Introduction

My family has persuaded me to write something about my wartime experiences. The problem is I am somewhat advanced in years and my memory is not as clear as it used to be. Consequently, some of my long-term memories may be economical with the truth. That is, the truth may have been embroidered out of all recognition. You, dear reader, have the task of deciding what is true in the sense of what actually happened and what is fiction. It's rather like the radio programme *The Unbelievable Truth*, in which panel members listen to a piece of prose and have to decide whether any facts in it are true. There is also the television programme *Would I Lie to You?* in which someone relates an experience from his or her life and the opposing panel has to decide whether it is true or a lie. There seems to be a strange zeitgeist in the present age because there is also a phenomenon called Fake News. Is what we hear or read on the various forms of media fact or fiction? How can you tell the difference?

Although this is an autobiographical account, some of it is fictitious. Whether what is written here is true or false hardly matters. The important thing is that a tale is being told. Who cares whether it is true? If any of the characters bear a resemblance to anyone living or dead, it is purely coincidental.

1

Behind Enemy Lines

I was crouching in the fuselage of a 1944 British Spitfire, bouncing over Germany towards Cologne. To be absolutely honest, I don't know whether it was a Spitfire. Aeroplanes are not my thing; they are simply a means of getting from A to B. All I know was this plane had been specially adapted to carry one passenger: me. My parachute kit rested on my back, and the noise of the engine was unrelenting. Conversation with the pilot and his navigator was impossible. I crouched there in silence, pondering my plight.

Most of the way, we managed to stay above the clouds and therefore out of sight of enemy searchlights. However, as we neared our destination and came below the clouds, we ran into a barrage of antiaircraft fire. The noise was intense, and the light from exploding shells peppered my vision. How we survived, I shall never know. Through all the exploding shells, I could just make out the wonderful, majestic spire of Cologne Cathedral standing proud, tall, and erect in the distance. It seemed to be a symbol of all that was good in the world standing in utter defiance of all that was bad. *Why is there so much evil in the world?* This was a very fleeting thought. The time wasn't exactly appropriate for a philosophical discussion on the problem of evil. It did occur to me, though, that if many people ask why there is so much suffering when God is a God of love, then I want ask, why is there so much good, so much self-sacrifice, and so much altruism if there isn't a God at all?

Very quickly I came back to the perils of the present moment. I was at the plane's door, the wind buffeting us, the noise screaming. I was on edge waiting for the green light, hoping and praying fervently I would survive the barrage. Sooner than expected, the red light turned to green.

'Off you go,' yelled the pilot. 'And good luck.'

The door opened, and I jumped into the murky unknown. My parachute was black, having been especially made for the occasion. I was almost impossible to pick out of the night sky. The day had also been selected because there was no moon at all. It was very, very dark. There was noise all around me, but I drifted steadily downwards. I realised the Spitfire had been hit and was hurtling towards the ground with a screaming sound that was enough to wake the dead. It seemed luck was with me and not with the pilot and his crew. My hope of landing undetected was now forlorn. The hunt would be on for the fallen plane and its crew.

Some things that happen in life seem to be providential. There is apparently no rhyme or reason; it's more like playing a game of cards. All you can do is play the hand you have been dealt. There is no way you can change the cards you have been dealt unless you cheat. You must, quite literally, get on with it and play the game. Some would argue that things don't happen by chance. For the Christian, at least, there is a God who protects us and looks after us. If so, how does one account for the many Christians who were killed in the war whereas others like me were unharmed? Can God be so capricious? Life seems more like a game of snakes and ladders. At the throw of the dice, you can be happily going up a ladder, but then at a second throw of the dice, your luck changes and down you fall on a snake. One might then ask, 'Why believe in God?' The point is how we react to the things that befall us. Christians believe that God is with them all the time, through thick and thin.

On this night, my cards were good. I didn't parachute onto the ground. The chute caught on some branches, and I managed to find some purchase on a large branch and stay there. It is difficult to be precise, but I must have been a good forty feet off the ground. This was all to the good because very soon I heard the sound of German voices below. They were searching for something or someone. I only heard them; I couldn't see anyone. It was pitch black except for some faint torchlight on the ground below. I couldn't even see my hand in front of my face. I hardly dared breathe, let alone move. Discretion being the better part of valour, I made up my mind to stay there, at least until daybreak.

After a long, long night, the day eventually arrived with a very watery sun; this was, after all, late summer. As the light increased, I could see there were still people on the ground below, and I could just make out their uniforms. Their colour clearly told me they were the German military. Again, as luck or providence would have it, I had landed in a forest amongst pine trees, but my parachute had wondrously found a solitary oak tree. This had still to shed its leaves, and I was sufficiently high up to remain undetected for the time being. Every intake of breath amongst the pines was like breathing in the smell of Christmas. For me, Christmas is associated with different smells but especially the smell of a pine tree. My thoughts drifted off to Christmas at home. In the middle of a war and food rationing, there had been little in the way of a Christmas dinner, but my family had managed to buy a small tree, which we'd decorated with a star and homemade paper baubles.

As day wore on, the voices below faded away. All I had for company were the birds singing and a particularly nosy and noisy magpie. I had to hope that the bird wouldn't attract attention from the voices below. My hip flask had managed to stay attached to my belt, and so I had a small supply of water to slake my thirst. Miraculously, a couple of Spam sandwiches remained intact in my pocket—somewhat squashed, but when you are in the predicament I was in, you will eat just about anything. And once the flask was empty, it doesn't take much imagination to realise what it was used for.

As night fell and I was once again enveloped in a thick blanket of darkness, I made the decision to descend to the ground. This was easier said than done. For over twelve hours, I had hardly moved, and my joints had stiffened up in the chill of the night air. Slowly but surely, I kept feeling my way and finding secure branches for my feet to rest on and take my weight. After what seemed an interminably long time, I stood on terra firma and gave the tree a mighty hug of thanks for the shelter it had afforded.

At that precise moment, there was a prod in my back that felt like the barrel of a gun. I froze. I didn't move an inch. I know it is a cliché, but my life really did flash before me. My heart sank into my boots. This was it. I had been discovered, and my mission (whatever it was to be) and my life had come to an end. What an ignominious way to terminate a life: killed by a bullet in the middle of a forest with nobody to mourn my passing. Then a small hand tugged at my shoulder and turned me round. Through the darkness, I could dimly discern not a soldier but the small figure of what I took to be a young lad. He was very slight of stature and no more than five feet in height. Holding a finger to his lips, he beckoned me to follow him. Silence was the order of the day. What choice did I have? Here I was, well behind enemy lines with no support and a single handgun. Was I to shoot him or follow him? Shooting was against my principles anyway, but was he friend or foe? Was he going to take care of me or hand me over to the military? How did he know I was there? Did he have eyes that could see in the dark? In reality, there was little choice. I followed him.

We picked our way very carefully and very quietly through the forest. How this young lad found the way at all was a mystery. I could barely see him leading the way, let alone see the path or any signposts. Where was I? All I knew for sure was that I was somewhere near Cologne. On we went through the night and through the forest. We trudged along quite slowly for what seemed like a couple of hours but in reality was probably about thirty minutes. Perhaps my pilot had lost his way and I was actually in an African jungle. Perhaps I hadn't seen Cologne Cathedral after all. My mind was beginning to wander, all sorts of flights of fancy beginning to take hold. Then we emerged into a clearing. We seemed to be on the outskirts of a small village.

I could just discern the outline of a church. That was where we were heading. On reaching the building, the young lad opened the side door with a key and led me downstairs into the basement. There was a door at one end which he unlocked and we went through. The lad switched on a small torch and motioned to me to sit down.

'I will be back in a few hours,' he said in very good English with hardly a trace of a German accent. He shut and locked the door and left me to my own devices.

With the aid of the torch, I could see a small wooden table with a few books on it, a cassock and preaching gown hanging on a coat stand, a sink with a solitary tap, and some cupboards. That was about it. I guessed I was in the church vestry, where the priest would robe before taking a service. I switched off the torch to preserve the battery. While sitting in the darkness, I pondered how on earth I had got myself into this mess.

2

In the Beginning

You may have guessed by now that I have a keen interest in religion. In actual fact, I was once a student of theology in the faculty of divinity at the University of Manchester. I received my call-up papers to go into the armed services in 1942 three years after the war had started. However, I immediately applied for exemption on the grounds of my religious beliefs. My father before me had been a conscientious objector in the Great War. It was very much frowned upon by the authorities, and one automatically had to spend time in jail. The public at large also derided anybody who refused to fight for his country, and so on coming out of prison, these people, who were nicked named conchies, found it very difficult to gain any kind of employment. My dad was an accountant by profession, so eventually he was able to work, but others were not quite so fortunate. Many a conversation I had with those who had not fought in the war on principle had a very hard life supporting their family. I can still hear my dad saying, 'I am a Christian. How can I kill anyone? It is completely against everything I believe in.'

My mum would sometimes respond by saying, 'What about me and the country? Aren't we worth defending?'

My dad always replied by talking about Donald Soper, a Methodist minister and a hero of his. 'I'm not the only to object to war. Look at Soper. He stands at Speaker's Corner in Hyde Park every Sunday and expounds his views on pacifism to anyone who will listen.'

'I wonder whether anyone does listen,' retorted Mum.

'They certainly do,' replied Dad, 'but of course some people vilify him for his stance. In fact, sometimes, Soper has to have police protection, but that doesn't deter him.'

The decision to become a pacifist was not a decision to be taken lightly. How ironic that here we were at war again, when the Great War was supposedly the war to end all wars. I wonder why it is that people often feel the only way to end a dispute is through violence. Is it a civilised, not to mention loving, action to drop bombs on innocent people?

To say war makes an indelible mark on people is something of an understatement. Vera Brittain had served as a nurse on the front line in France during the Great War. Her brother and fiancé had both been killed in action. Apart from nursing the British injured, she found herself nursing some wounded German soldiers. How poignant, she thought, that she was tending their wounds so that they would be fit enough to go into battle again and probably get killed. Her experiences, which she wrote about in a book called *The Testament of Youth*, lead Vera Brittain into being a confirmed pacifist.

Each morning was something of a trial as I waited for the post to arrive. I knew it was only a matter of time before my call-up papers arrived. As sure as eggs are eggs, the fateful day arrived, and the letter landed with a thud on the doormat. The conscription board I was required to attend was very demanding. I was ushered into a very austere room with portraits of former service personnel in uniform with all their medals, glaring down at us. The interview panel was comprised of five people, four men and a woman. One of them motioned me to sit down, but nothing was said for at least two minutes. They scrutinised me from top to bottom, completely poker-faced. I felt as though I was facing a cold brick wall. My nerves began to jangle. I realised there would be no possibility of bluffing my way through. My arguments to support my belief in pacifism would need to be very good. I felt reasonably confident because being a theology student I knew the Bible fairly well.

The silence was suddenly broken. There were no social niceties of any kind, only an abrupt question. 'Mr Rothwell, tell us why you think you are a pacifist,' said one of the panel.

'Jesus requires his followers to love their enemies and pray for those who persecute them,' I said. 'Furthermore, the prime commandment in the New Testament is to love other people, not to kill them, even if one may be tempted to do so. Even in the Old Testament, one of the Ten Commandments is "Thou shalt not kill".'

I felt I was just getting into my stride when I was quickly interrupted by the lady on the panel. 'But what if your country is invaded? Isn't it important to defend ourselves, even if it means using force?'

'Of course that is a perfectly reasonable view,' I replied, 'but I think it flies in the face of the teaching of Jesus. I know full well St Augustine developed a theory of the just war, but this still seems to contravene what Jesus requires of his followers: a nonviolent approach to whatever befalls us. Not only that, but for me personally, it would be difficult to follow the orders of my commanding officer. The teaching of Jesus is that we cannot serve two masters. I would react very adversely if I was ordered to do something that directly contravened my principles as a Christian. How is it possible to serve two masters?'

Apart from quoting liberally from the New Testament, I was also able to mention the experiences of Vera Brittain and Donald Soper. Naturally, my interrogation didn't stop there. Far from it. One of the male panellists fixed his eyes on me, rested his chin on his hands, and retorted, 'If your nearest and dearest is attacked, are you going to stand by and let them get on with it?'

I was ready for this question simply because it is always asked of those who would purport to be a pacifist. 'I would do all in my power to prevent the attack, but I would not kill the attacker. How can I pray for my brothers or sisters and at the same time kill them? Isn't that surely a contradiction in terms?'

The interviewer wasn't satisfied. 'Wouldn't you be prepared to defend your country against an aggressor?'

'I would certainly be prepared to engage in nonviolent resistance and make life as difficult as possible for the enemy. However, killing other people is simply something I cannot countenance.'

After another prolonged period of silence, during which I felt I my very thoughts were being read, I was asked to leave the room.

A couple of days later, much to my relief, a letter arrived stating that my request to abstain from military service had been granted. I must have defended my position with complete conviction. However, my final statement about nonviolent resistance was to prove my undoing.

Some weeks later, I was in the theology faculty library, quietly reading and getting to grips with a theological tome, when a gentleman approached me. He was not the kind of person who would stand out in a crowd. Quite the opposite. He was nondescript. He had no distinguishing features like a beard or red hair or even no hair at all. His clothes were remarkable for their lack of style and colour. If anything stood out about this guy, it was the fact that nothing stood out! He whispered that he wanted a word with me, and so we retired to the faculty refectory. The tea was like coloured water, but the conversation was somewhat more enlivening. My hair began to stand up on end, and goose pimples covered my arms.

It transpired that this anonymous looking man worked for the secret service. At least, that was what he said, and who was I to disbelieve him? As a result of my interrogation a few weeks earlier, my forms had been passed on to the service. They had noticed I had learnt German at school, and one of my hobbies was trying to solve cryptic crosswords.

'Malcolm,' the man said, 'we would like you to attend a very special selection conference in a few days' time. If successful, you will then give up your studies and work for us on a variety of different assignments, but most probably in Germany.'

I was speechless, or as they say in my part of the world, gobsmacked. To be taken from the hallowed walls of a faculty of divinity with the prospect of being thrown into the maelstrom of war behind enemy lines was daunting and very frightening, to say the least. When I had recovered from the shock, I was able to blurt out, 'When does the selection process take place, and where does it happen?'

'The process takes place in Manchester town hall in a week's time,' the nondescript man replied.

As I tried to regain my composure I found myself agreeing to accept his invitation. Did I have any choice?

I had no difficulty locating the town hall or being on time. My dad worked within those impressive Gothic walls, and I had sometimes visited him there, so I almost felt at home. There were about two dozen of us, men and women, all seated at single desks. The man whom I had met a week earlier was in charge of the process, and the first thing he asked us to do was complete a cryptic crossword puzzle as quickly as possible. Even now, years later, I can still remember one or two of the clues.

'Do you know a backward boy in the Lake District?' Easy. (Answer: Kendal.) 'Not usually thought of as a composer of small beer.' (Answer: Elgar.) 'Rides with mother having an outside attempt.' (Answer: bridesmaid.) And so on. I was by no means the fastest, but I did manage to complete the puzzle in a fairly decent time. I was then taken to one side, and a couple of people asked me a few questions about my life. What was my German like? Did I have any family or close friends? What sort of nonviolent resistance did I envisage? Did I have any experience keeping secrets? I really can't remember the answers because my heart was racing away, but I do remember asking one particular question.

'If I should be selected, what sort of training would I have to go through?' To be honest, I didn't fancy training of any sort, let along military training.

'You will be required to go to a secret location, where you will be given various codes to decipher. We will write to you with the details in a few days.'

I felt reasonably reassured. I did like puzzles of any kind.

Some days later, there was a knock at the door, and a letter was handed over by special delivery. On the back were printed the words 'On His Majesty's Service'. It could only mean one thing. With trembling hands, I fumbled my way into the envelope. The letter inside was brief and to the point. I had been selected to serve in His Majesty's secret service, and could I appear at somewhere called Bletchley Park in a week's time. Could I also immediately destroy the letter? This was my first introduction into the secrecy of my new way of life.

I had not the faintest idea where Bletchley Park was, and so my first task was to find a map of England and then plan how I was going to get there. I discovered that the venue was somewhere north of London. Travelling by car wasn't an option because I didn't have one. Train seemed to be the only answer. I was impatient—one of my many faults—but the journey seemed to take forever. There wasn't a through train, so I had to change at Birmingham, New Street, and Watford Junction. Each train was full of military personnel, either travelling home on leave or going to their next billet. The difference between the two was obvious. Those travelling home looked tired, drawn, and in some cases injured. I have to say I felt a tinge of guilt that I wasn't also in uniform, but at least I was doing my bit in defence of the country—although what that bit was, I hadn't yet found out.

There was nothing remarkable about Bletchley Park. The most apt word to describe it was nondescript. It was in the middle of nowhere and consisted of a few rows of wooden huts with nothing to distinguish between them except a number on the main door. In each hut, there were either rows of desks or whirring machinery. The desks were mostly inhabited by girls clicking away on typewriters, and the machinery was attended by young men. This was my first sight of a computer—a great pile of whirring cog wheels which filled the whole room. How did anyone know how to work such a machine? Machines have never meant much to me. As a small boy, I was given a Meccano set, but it hardly saw the light of day; I didn't seem to have that kind of brain. Those in charge quickly realised I was in the wrong place, and so I was placed amongst the girls to work out some code or other. This was much more my line of business, and it was much more congenial. There were, after all, some good-looking girls in the bunch. I thought it wouldn't be long before I plucked up courage and asked one of them out for a drink in the local pub. Unfortunately, that was not to be.

After a few weeks deciphering various codes, I was again approached by an anonymous-looking man. 'Could you spare a few moments?'

Again, I didn't feel as though there was any choice. My first thought was I wasn't up to the required standard and was going to be posted elsewhere. Whether I was up to standard or not, I shall never know because the man carried on talking.

'You are being sent to North Wales, where you will undergo a certain amount of arduous physical training. You'll also have some tuition to bring your German up to scratch.'

I confessed to being somewhat worried about the thought of physical training.

'You have nothing to worry about. You are quite young and fairly fit.'

I felt reasonably reassured, although I doubted his assessment of my fitness. I was not in a position to argue the point and was left wondering just how arduous the training was going to be.

3

Finding My Bearings

My daydreaming seemed to go on forever. After all, in that cold, dark vestry, there was nothing else to do. The door was locked. The cupboards were locked. I daren't switch on the lights for fear of being discovered. In fact, I was fearful of moving in case I made a noise. That was the problem: having no idea of where I was or whether people lived roundabout, or even if there was a church service about to take place. Would the priest, or whatever he called himself, suddenly descend and demand to know what was going on? Would my German be up to it? Was the lad who brought me here friend or foe? Would he betray me? Would I ever eat again? Was this my last day on earth? There were many questions and no answers—very frustrating.

My dreaming came to an abrupt halt. The key in the door rattled, and in came a body. I quickly switched on my torch and discovered it to be the small person who had brought me there. At least, I assumed it was.

'My name is Ingeborg,' she said in impeccable English, 'but everyone calls me Inge.'

'I thought you were a boy,' I replied, feeling slightly embarrassed. She was wearing a dark jacket and dark slacks, and this, coupled with the fact that her hair was concealed by a beret, made my mistake quite easy to understand. At least, that was what I told myself.

She smiled a knowing smile, as though she was quite used to being mistaken for a boy. 'I've brought something for you to eat and drink,' she said, 'but you must stay here for a little longer until we are sure that all the soldiers have gone. I will come again in a few hours' time.' With that, she was gone and I was left to my own devices.

Without a moment's hesitation, I opened the small food parcel that Inge had brought me. To be brutally honest, I was shocked. My idea of food under such circumstances would be a tasty sandwich, although not too tasty given all the food rationing that was going on. The bread would be soft and white and easy to digest. German bread is quite different, and this was my first introduction to it. German bread, or at least that which I had been given, was hard and black and tasted of rye. My teeth were not in very good shape, and it took me all my time to chew one small section. Every bite felt like a meal in itself. In comparison, English bread can only be described as cotton wool. However, one has to be thankful for small mercies. As I chomped away, I reflected on the fact that I was still alive and was not going to be betrayed. If that was the case, soldiers would have appeared long since. My spirits began to lift.

Sometime later—how much later, I have no way of knowing; the passage of time had ceased to have any meaning—the door opened again. This time, the profile of a much larger figure appeared in the doorway. My heart missed a beat. Could I have been betrayed after all? Had I been lulled into a false sense of security? Again came the order: 'Follow me.' I felt like a lamb to the slaughter but did as I was told. A brief consideration of my options had rapidly come to the conclusion there weren't any other options. On exiting the church, I discovered that night had fallen. We walked quickly and quietly along a narrow path on the edge of the forest until we came upon a house. We entered the house, which I could see was quite old and rustic in nature. I was taken downstairs into the cellar.

'My name is Karl,' the man said, 'and I am Inge's father. I am also the priest.' His English was not quite as good as his daughter's; he spoke with a slight accent. Not that it mattered. Apparently, I was safe. 'I am a member of the German resistance. It is an anti-Nazi movement. You will be safe here for a little while.'

This came as a complete shock. I had heard of the French, Polish, and Greek resistance, but I had no idea a German resistance existed. 'Are there many of you?' I asked, feeling quite excited and relieved.

'Now is not the time for your questions. For the moment, be content. We will talk later. I have left a little food and water, but you must understand food is in very short supply.' With that, he left me to survey my surroundings. One thing was quite clear: war or no war, there were more than a few bottles of wine stored on the racks round the wall. Should the occasion arise, there was plenty of scope for a memorable celebration. I had a comfortable chair to sit on, thankfully, and apart from an assortment of gardening tools and a lot of empty preserving jars, there was little else. There was ample time for my own thoughts.

Some people find it very difficult to sit quietly; they have to be up and about, busy doing things. It was a challenge for me as well. Although I was not married and so didn't have a family to worry about, there was always another essay to write. Student life can be quite demanding at times. Whilst preparing for an essay on early Christianity, I came across the following quote, which I can barely remember except that it was written by an anonymous, fourth-century monk.

'Unless there is a still centre in the middle of the storm, unless a person in the midst of all their activities preserves a secret room in their heart where they stand alone before God, unless we do this we will lose all sense of spiritual direction and be torn to pieces.'

I was desperately in need of finding that still centre here in the cellar with nothing but a deep, deep silence to accompany me. I certainly had no wish to be torn to pieces. Something else also came to mind: a piece of advice which I didn't take much notice of at the time. My tutor had said that if things started to go downhill, I should take things a day at a time. A day at a time! I was taking things a minute at a time. Any moment, things could change for the better or for the worse. One thing was certain: I was not in control of the future. Is anybody? We like to think we are in control, but the reality is that at any time, things can take a turn for the worse or for the better.

Deep breaths were the order of the day. I discovered that by concentrating on my breathing, I was brought into the present moment, and I found myself feeling very peaceful. Some might argue that is precisely where they find God, in the present moment. After all, the only reality is what we experience in the here and now. Never mind the past, which has gone and can't be undone, or the future, which has yet to be determined. Simply dwell in the reality of the present moment. I have no idea how long I was in this state of contemplation. All I know is I was filled with a deep sense of peace and tranquillity.

This came to an end rather abruptly when Inge entered the cellar. Immediately, I could see why she had worn a beret. She had beautiful blonde hair that fell to her shoulders like the mane of a lion. She was slightly built and had not yet developed into a fully grown woman. I guessed that she was about 16 or 17 years old. As long as her hair remained invisible, she could easily be mistaken for a young lad.

'I'm very sorry we have neglected you,' she said, 'but we didn't want to attract any attention.'

'Where am I?' I asked.

'You are in a very small village called Kleineichen, which is about eight kilometres from the centre of Köln.'

'Kleineichen,' I repeated. 'Doesn't that mean little oak?'

'It does indeed.'

'Well, I think I must have sat in it last night, but now, thankfully, it is no longer a little oak. It is a great big oak.'

'That is how I found you. If you had landed in any of the pine trees, you would immediately have been seen because, as you know, pine trees are very slender and have no branches near the ground. We are surrounded by a thick, pine forest called Königsforst, and the nearest small town in the opposite direction to Köln is called Rösrath. I think you have already seen some of the forest.'

Before I could reply, she went on to say that the village consisted of a few dwellings, a church, a farm, and an inn about one kilometre away on the Rösrather straße, the main road between the city and Rösrath. The church also included a small convent, which was home to a few Catholic sisters. She said her father was the priest of the village church along with two other nearby village communities.

'Do you say priest? Or vicar? Or pastor?' She said.

'Let's just say minister,' I said.

Inge had a lovely, sing-song, melodious voice which I could have listened to all day.

'How is it that your English is so good?' I inquired.

'I learn English at school, but also my parents spent a few holidays in England before this wretched war, and I always went with them. I will let them tell you about their English connection. Papa will come and talk to you as soon as he has time. I'm very sorry we have to keep you in the cellar, but because he is a minister and well-known in the area, he has visits from all sorts of different people. We never know who is going to knock at the door, and it is very important that you are not seen. Word could quickly get round the village, and that would not be very good at all.'

I nodded. They obviously had things sorted out between them, so who was I to argue? Inge left, but not without leaving a supply of black bread and some sauerkraut. For some reason, I didn't have any appetite. My desire was to fulfil my mission and ask Karl some important questions. How did they know where to find me? Did they know what my mission was? What was their English connection? How long could I stay there? Could they tell me about the German resistance? Questions, questions. Perhaps answers would come in due course. For the time being, I reflected on my training, which had supposedly prepared me for this moment.

4

North Wales

The anonymous-looking man had said before sending me anywhere in Germany, a certain amount of training was necessary. Consequently, I found myself on a train heading towards North Wales, to a small village called Penmaenmawr. The village is situated on the North Wales coast between Conwy and Llanfairfechan. The village was built up around the quarry industry, and it was also a small tourist resort because of its really good sandy beach. On arriving at the station, I was met by an aide-de-camp and driven up the hill to a large house called Bryn; I later discovered that the word is Welsh for hill or mound. Bryn, it turns out, used to be a Christian Endeavour Holiday Home where like-minded people could spend their annual holidays, walking, playing tennis, putting on concerts, and generally enjoying their time together. The house had been requisitioned by the army for training purposes. (I have recently discovered that Bryn still exists but has now been turned into apartments). I had no initial complaints. Bryn was a notable Victorian villa with a comfortable lounge and sun lounge, with views over the bay to Puffin Island and the south-eastern tip of Anglesey on the western side; over to the north-east was the limestone headland of the Great Orme. There was also a dining room downstairs that had been converted into a more practical canteen. Upstairs were married quarters and rooms for officers. I was billeted in another large room round the back opposite, a shed-like building with the word 'Morgue' on it. *Did people die here?* I wondered, feeling slightly uncomfortable. *Is the training so arduous? What have I let myself in for?*

I bunked down with three other guys who were similar in age to me but were more experienced in the ways of the army. They had served for a number of years and were now involved with this training because they had also been assigned for special duties. There was big Barrett, well over six feet tall. I never thought to ask him where that strange name came from. All I knew was that his legs seemed to come up to his armpits. He was very amiable, chatty, and helpful; he could engage in conversation with anybody at any time and seemed to have an endless supply of tales to tell. I'm not too sure how he managed to be there at all because he clearly had a default in one of his eyes. Then there was Henry. What a live wire he was! Always on the move, always ready for action. He was small, fit, athletic, and very hairy. Henry was a complete extrovert. The final guy was Spencer. He was quite different, much more studious and thoughtful, but somehow he was very steady and reassuring. Some might say he was ponderous, but he had a heart of gold and a dry sense of humour. These three were to be my close companions for the next six weeks. Barrett, Henry, and Spencer had been sent here, like me, to do some hard physical training, although I was not sure what their specific roles were. We were known by other residents of Bryn as the four musketeers.

After a couple of days settling in and getting to know our officers, as well as what was expected of us, the exercises began. Our first task was to walk as fast as we could straight up the mountain behind us. This took us up the Green Gorge, which was quite aptly named, and along to a stone circle that was known locally as the Druid's Circle. Our ordinance survey map informed us the mountain in the background was Tal Y Fan. The map also specified that the circle was an ancient burial chamber. Barrett, the mine of information, told us it was a prehistoric stone circle built around 1450–1400 BC. My fascination with the spirituality of ancient people was partly sparked off by this ancient monument. What kind of religious rituals did ancient men and women engage in? What did they believe about the nature of the world? Looking across the bay, one had a good view of Puffin Island, where a monk called Seiriol had lived in the sixth century. Why would a people go live in complete isolation, away from civilisation? Were they called by God to live such a life, or were they just very antisocial? More to the point, how did they survive, particularly in winter? What did they eat? Wandering thoughts such as these made the walk down seem much quicker, and I even managed to keep up with my three comrades; Spencer was struggling to keep up as well.

The following day, we began the same walk as previously, but instead of going straight up the gorge, we turned a sharp left along Jubilee walk. We walked between two vertical pillars, on one of which was a plaque stating the path had been opened in 1888 in memory of Queen Victoria's jubilee the previous year. This is a lovely, gentle stroll round the mountain at the back of the town, and it naturally gives wonderful views over the whole of the bay and Conwy Mountain towards the east. I guess we were being broken in very gently because there was plenty of time for conversation and getting to know each other. As it happened, all four of us were from Lancashire, and so we all spoke the same language! One can imagine our chatter often revolved around girls, and it transpired that big Barrett and Spencer were already engaged. They even had time to show off some photographs of their fiancées. Henry and I had not yet been hitched and were still shopping around, as one might say.

'Your time will come,' shouted Barrett.

'Not me,' I replied. 'I'm not getting married. I like being single.'

'We've all said that once upon a time,' came Spencer's dry remark. 'Then just as we looked the other way, we got hooked.'

For once, Henry kept very quiet. He was usually the one to jump into a conversation, but this time he held his own counsel.

Upon coming to the end of the Jubilee walk, we dropped down a gorge called Fairy Glen, although why it had that name, I had no idea. Barrett didn't know either; he was fallible after all. Needless to say, we didn't come across any fairies. The path was through a thickly wooded area and was not only steep but quite slippery and rocky. We emerged at the bottom into a village called Dwygyfylchi, which is impossible for an Englishman to pronounce, so we just called it Dirty Filthy. We then walked back along the road into Penmaenmawr. The walk had been relatively short and simple, and so on our return, our superiors had arranged for a session of weight training to keep us on our toes. Life was by no means a bed of roses.

On another day, we took the train into Conwy, the next station down the line. Unfortunately, time didn't allow us to wander round the ancient Edwardian Conwy castle because our task was to walk through the town and take the path up Conwy Mountain. Although it was called a mountain, it was hardly that, being only 801 feet high. Nevertheless, the mountain is quite steep, and again wonderful views over the bay are afforded. Once at the top, we quickly descended down to the old Conwy Road to Penmaenmawr Road via the Sychnant Pass. We paused for breath when we reached the pass, and a strange thing happened. We found ourselves standing in front of a very large rock and realised that our voices were being echoed across the valley. Henry, being the joker in the pack, suggested we all shout, 'What would you do if your wife drank liquor?' This we did with one great voice, and of course, the answer echoed back: 'Lick 'er.' Such were the silly things that made our days seem lighter and more manageable.

The four of us were beginning to get fitter and wake up the following morning without feeling stiff. Our final short outing was a long run along the beach with a heavy load on. This is not as easy as it sounds. On wet sand, your calves soon tighten up, and you know you have your work cut out to complete the task. However, we managed about five miles of such running and were so delighted that we completed the day by running naked into the sea. There was no one around, and even if they had been, we were too exhausted to worry about it. The coolness of the sea was wonderfully restoring, so much so that we were able to jog back up the hill to Bryn.

When we weren't outdoors trying to keep fit, an instructor trained us in how to load and use a revolver. This was not my cup of tea by any stretch of the imagination. I would aim at the target and shut my eyes, hoping I wouldn't be too far off the mark. The thought of actually killing somebody, even if they were the enemy, was completely anathema to me. We were also instructed in silent man-to-man combat. I could just about stomach this, and I became quite skilled at disabling my opponent without actually killing him. Every minute of every day seemed to be filled with one activity or another. I could only presume that one day all this effort would prove to have been useful.

5

Some Answers

Inge's papa, Karl, was a man in his early fifties. He had a slight figure and would have been quite good looking in his youth, but the ravages of war had taken their toll. His face had the wrinkles of many former smiles, but now his face bore the wrinkles of anxiety and hunger. He had a shock of thick, unruly white hair which gave him the air of an academic. Somehow, I could imagine him preaching from the church pulpit, but his style would not be loud and bombastic; he would be there to encourage, comfort, and support his flock. He spoke very softly and in very good English but with an obvious accent. Before saying anything, he shook my hand. I was later to discover that Germans often did this. They shook hands at the drop of a hat.

'I need to tell you a little bit about myself. My English is not very good, so I hope you can understand me.' I was all ears. What was he going to say?

'My wife and I went on holiday to England about twenty years ago, after World War I. We were invited to attend an international week at a Christian Holiday Home in Kent's Bank in the Lake District. Apart from us Germans, there were young men and women of various nationalities. They were not all Christians. Towards the end of spending two weeks together, it became apparent that we wanted to put into words our commitment to peace and to working together. We felt we were all brothers and sisters. You could say we were all comrades. Yes, we were all quite young and very idealistic, but sometimes you have to reach for the stars; otherwise you only achieve very ordinary things. I think you have a saying: "Your reach must exceed your grasp, otherwise what is a heaven for?"'

I sat enthralled by Karl's story.

'The vision we decided goes something like this: "Mankind is one great brotherhood, indivisible alike by religion, nationality, or colour, with God being the father of all. Our aim is to try to destroy those things which separate people from each other, to do away with the occasion of wars, and to put in their place some kind of loving fellowship."'

'That sounds all very well and good,' I said. 'But here we are at war, and presumably you are a soldier.'

'I was in the military,' he affirmed. 'But whilst on duty in Greece, I was wounded in my leg. I had to make my way back to Germany—sometimes on foot, sometimes with the help of the Greek resistance. Finally, I managed to jump onto a goods train. The journey back from Greece took about ten days.'

Now I knew why Karl always walked with a slight limp.

'But why did you serve as a soldier at all? What about your vision of mankind being one great brotherhood?'

His answer was brief and to the point. 'If we don't serve in the military, we are shot.'

'That is reason enough for anybody,' I said, feeling quite stupid for being so naive.

'Although it was really painful, I was actually very glad to be wounded because that gave me an excuse to come home and get away from all the violence. Since returning, I have contacted, mainly through my church connections, a few people who are against the Nazis. This is very dangerous because, as you can imagine, if we are found out, then we shall be shot without question. There is usually one person in each village who can be relied upon.

'There is one other thing I need to say. I am so sorry the food we give you is not very interesting. You must understand that food is very short here. I try to grow my own, and as you see from all the jars in this room, we try to preserve as much as we can. As it happens, my wife, Ursula, is a watch and clock repairer, and so she is able to do some repairs for people in return for which they give us some vegetables. One man in particular keeps us supplied with carrots and potatoes.

'Our other source of food is England,' he added. 'The friends, the comrades we met up with so many years ago, have been kind enough to send us care packages. These arrive about once a month and give us great encouragement. It is good to feel part of this international brotherhood even though we are at war. I hope this answers some of your questions. Now, you must tell me about yourself.'

I briefly explained to Karl my pacifism and horror of violence but how I had been selected into special services because of my German.

'Ha-ha, wir können Deutsch sprechen!' he quickly interjected.

I shook my head. 'Your English is far better than my German. Let's carry on as we are.'

In hindsight, that was probably a wrong decision. It would greatly have helped my cause if my German had improved, and here was a wonderful opportunity. Isn't hindsight a wonderful thing? I carried on with my story, telling him a little bit about my training in North Wales.

'Ich kann es kaum glauben,' Karl said, smiling. 'My wife and I actually stayed in Bryn in the twenties for a holiday. We have many happy memories and made many friends. They are the ones who send us care packets.'

Extraordinary! I found it difficult to believe as well. Apparently, I had trained in a place where Karl and his wife had spent their holiday. How unlikely was that? I felt we were almost related. What a prescient feeling. I began to wonder what other surprises were in store.

My curiosity about Karl's wife was aroused. Nothing had been said about her or the rest of his family. Furthermore, Inge had slipped out that she had two younger brothers. Did they know I was in their cellar? What if they suddenly found me? The inner voice of doubt began to make its presence felt.

6

More Training

I have to admit one could easily think that up to this moment we were tourists having a good time. Yes, we had undergone some physical training, but it could hardly be called strenuous. The situation was about to change dramatically. In the morning at first light, the four of us were commanded to walk up Snowdon with a full pack.

There were various ways up the mountain, but the chosen route was along the Pyg Track, probably so called after the nearby Pen Y Gwryd hotel. This route suited me fine because it was the track with the least ascent. The track starts from the Pen y Pass, which is already quite high up. The path was quite rocky and steep to begin with, but we managed to ascend without any difficulty. We came to the top of the first bit and stopped for a breather.

'You see that steep, rocky path there?' Barrett said, pointing with his finger. 'That is called Crib Goch, and at the top it is like a knife's edge.'

'Probably like Striding Edge in the Lake District,' interjected Spencer.

'I fancy Crib Goch,' blurted out Henry.

'Let's just do what we've been ordered to do,' I implored. 'I have no doubt Crib Goch will feature somewhere in our training.'

There was no discussion, and so we pressed on along an almost straight path which offered views to the miner's track below and two beautiful shimmering lakes. The final ascent was quite steep and slippery, so we really had to watch our footing. Finally, we reached the top but not the summit. That was another stretch which took us alongside the famous Snowdon railway, which Barrett told us had been running since 1876. He was a gold mine of local information.

In spite of our loads, we managed to reach the summit in less than three hours. Snowdon, at over three thousand feet, is the highest mountain in Wales, but naturally it was shrouded in clouds, so there was no view at all. Not that we were there to admire the view. Our next task was to run down the Ranger path as quickly as possible to the jeep that would be waiting for us at the bottom. The four of us were down in just under thirty minutes. Remarkable. We were getting fitter by the minute—but there was to be no respite.

The next day we were told to climb the mountain called Tryfan, in the Ogwen Valley. I was later to discover that this mountain was a favourite amongst rock climbers, and in fact Edmond Hilary and his friends were to use this very same mountain as preparation for their ascent on Everest. All this was in the future. For the moment, I and my three friends had to find our way up the mountain. From the roadside, this mountain looks very, very steep and has the shape of an enormous fin. You have to climb or scramble right from the start. There is no easy bit as there is on the Pyg Track. Going up the North Ridge, you pass something call the Milestone Buttress and a rock jutting out of the mountainside that, for obvious reasons, is called the Canon Stone. You know you have reached the summit when you see two vertical columns of rock. My friends told me these were called Adam and Eve. If you jump across the four-foot gap, then legend has it you are given the Freedom of Tryfan. For me, discretion was the better part of valour, and I did not jump this so-called leap of faith. In my more meditative moments—and this was not one of them—I wonder why more people don't take the leap of faith into Christianity. Is it fear of the unknown? A fear of commitment? Perhaps they never get to that stage in their life. They never reach that part of the mountain. Life remains very flat and boring. Who knows?

It was a relief to discover that the descent was slightly easier. According to our OS map, we came down via Bylch Tryfan and the beautiful Llyn Bochlwyd before going back to the Ogwen Valley. One had to be careful coming down to not start an avalanche of stones and rocks. Some of the screes we scrambled down were very loose. Although Tryfan was not quite as high as Snowdon, the whole climb with full pack was very exhilarating and rewarding. The downside was the effect on my knees as a result of the very steep and speedy descent.

I couldn't help wondering what all this hard physical training was for. Yes, I was getting fit, but was I going to be climbing mountains in Germany? Of course, in the service you soon learn to not ask questions—you simply have to like it or lump it. This was very difficult for me because I was brought up to ask questions. Why? When? How? These were my favourite words, and they still are. In particular, I like to ask questions about the Christian faith. If we have been given brains, as we all have, then our duty is to use them. We are, after all, exhorted to believe with the heart and soul *and mind*. The trouble is that when people begin to question, Christians are often the first to complain and even refute the facts. Copernicus, Newton, Darwin, and Freud, to mention a few, have challenged the Christian faith by pushing the boundaries of our knowledge. The Church has resisted. Even now, there are some people who believe that the earth is flat or that the theory of evolution is false, in spite of all the evidence to the contrary.

One fact was absolutely certain: I was in the middle of training. The next day was a further challenge to my fitness. This time we had to complete the Snowdon Horseshoe. The beginning of our route took us over the first part of the Pyg Track, but instead of going straight on, at one point we turned sharp right and climbed almost vertically over Crib Goch. This walk is notorious for being more of a scramble than a walk. The route is along a knife's edge which can only be described as serrated. There is a precipice on both sides, and one is reduced to hands and knees at some points. I should also mention that the weather was very bad. In fact, it had rained nonstop since we'd left Pen-y-Pass. *How did I get myself into this mess?* I kept asking myself. We were cold and wet through, and hardly a word passed between us. We were in mortal danger of falling to our deaths because the rocks were really slippery; we had to concentrate all the time. One false move would have been fatal. We laboured on over Crib y Ddysgal, and we joined the top end of the Pyg Track, walked along the railway again, and went up to the summit, where we had a short break.

The second half of the route over the horseshoe was much easier. We went over Y Lliwedd fairly quickly and descended down a lot of loose rock and scree to our starting point at Pen-y-Pass. Job done. Yes, we were all very tired, but we were relieved that we had not sustained any major injuries, just some nasty blisters. The problem with the blisters was that we had one more walk to do on the morrow. This time we were taken to Bethsaida, a small town at the foot of the Ogwen Valley. Our task was to make our way over the Carnedd range of mountains all the way back to Penmaenmawr. The exercise this time was made more difficult because we had not been given our compasses. Again, the weather was very misty, and I had to admit we were finding it difficult to orientate ourselves. However, after a couple of hours walking, we bumped into a local shepherd, who pointed us in the right direction. If we had carried on in the same direction, we would have been in serious trouble. I wondered whether luck played a part in our lives.

There is the Chinese story of a farmer who used an old horse to till his fields. One day the horse escaped into the hills, and when the farmer's neighbours sympathised with the old man over his bad luck, the farmer replied, 'Bad luck? Good luck? Who knows?' A week later, the horse returned with a herd of horses from the hills, and this time the neighbours congratulated the farmer on his good luck. His reply was, 'Good luck? Bad luck? Who knows?' Then when the farmer's son was attempting to tame one of the wild horses, he fell off its back and broke his leg.

Everyone thought this was very bad luck. Not the farmer, whose only reaction was, 'Bad luck? Good luck? Who knows?' Some weeks later, the army marched into the village and conscripted every able-bodied youth they found. When they saw the farmer's son with his broken leg, they let him off. Now, was that good luck? Bad luck? Who knows?

The story, by Anthony de Mello, is one to ponder and savour. All I can say is I think it was good luck we met the farmer who told us which way to go, but who knows? The walk itself was uninteresting, with no views of note when the mist eventually lifted. No rock scrambles, just mile after mile of soft, boggy ground. Eventually, we reached the Druid's Circle, and then I knew we were nearly home. The four of us, who were by now best mates and well bonded, had a little bet on as to who would be first down to Bryn. We raced down Green Gorge. I'm not sure who won; I just know it wasn't me.

7

Tension Mounts

All that training and fresh air in Snowdonia seemed a million miles away as I sat alone in the cellar, wondering what would happen next. I didn't have to wait long. The door opened, and in walked the lady of the house. This was Ursula, and she was very neat and precisely dressed. I could imagine her sitting at her desk and gazing through a magnifying glass as she tried to repair the intricacies of a watch or clock. She came across as very warm-hearted, but in this moment of time she was also very tense.

'I am very sorry,' she said. 'We shall have to move you.' I noted this was another German who spoke almost impeccable English.

'Is there a problem?' I inquired. I did not relish the thought of moving. Precisely how long I was there escapes me. All I know is I felt I was getting used to my surroundings and almost beginning to feel at home.

'One of my sons has just rushed in to say the Gestapo are in the next village making house-to-house searches. You are in great danger if you stay here.'

The thought of the Gestapo, interrogation, and possible torture made my flesh creep. Where could I go that would be safe, away from prying eyes and ears? The answer came quickly.

'You are to go back to the church for a few days. In fact, there is a well-hidden room in the convent next to the church. No one will look there, but you will have to remain in darkness. I will take you there as soon as it is dark.'

As soon as darkness fell, Ursula took me to the convent. I could just about make out the name of the lane we went down: Nonnenweg—nuns way. Not a word was spoken. On arriving at the convent, she handed over me over to one of the sisters and said she would be back in two days. Why Ursula was doing this, I had no idea. Where were Inge and Karl?

Why hadn't I been put in the picture? Had they been betrayed? Where were the sons? There was more than enough time to wonder about these things. The two days passed very slowly. They seemed like a lifetime—all the time in the world for my imagination to run riot. My days were very briefly interrupted when one of the nuns brought me some food and drink. Nothing could have prepared me for what was to come. At times, the silence was deafening. I felt like shouting to the rooftops, 'Get me out of here!' It was almost like the cry of dereliction: 'Why have you deserted me?' Well, it wasn't really. I did feel abandoned, but I was not in pain and wasn't hungry, especially if I ate the pumpernickel. It is amazing how the darkness plays tricks with one's mind. *Did I hear a noise? Is that a light somewhere in the distance? Have I really a pain in my stomach? Do I need a doctor? Why can't I go to sleep? Can I hear some mice scratching* around? If only I could have a nice cup of tea.

My heart jumped a beat. There *was* a noise. People talking? This was it. I had been discovered. My assignment would never be completed. Never again would I see the white cliffs of Dover.

Slowly the door opened, and I could just make out the figure of Inge.

'Hello,' she said. 'I've just come to keep you company for a little while.'

'You are very kind. I was feeling a bit lonely,' I blurted out.

'I also needed to talk to somebody for a little while. I am fed up not only with this war but also with living at home. I'm fed up with my parents. Sometimes I wish they were dead.'

To say I was shocked at this outburst would be something of an understatement. Furthermore, we were sitting in complete darkness, and all I could hear was this kind of disembodied voice going on about her parents. I didn't know what to say, and because there was nowhere for me to go, I simply sat and listened.

'I'm sick of being at my parents' convenience. If something needs to be done, it always seems to be me who is asked, not my brothers. I don't feel anybody understands what I am going through. My parents keep asking me questions, and it irritates me. Why can't they leave me alone? Why do I seem to be holding a grudge against them? I seem to get along with everybody else. It's just them. It's like something bad is inside me, and they always manage to trigger it off, and I explode. How do you say it? Fly off the handle.'

I nodded but then realised that was a silly thing to do in the dark, so I gave an affirmative sound instead. She carried on like a waterfall in full spate.

'They are so controlling. They want me to do just what they want and never anything I want. Papa especially expects me to be just like him and won't accept that I have different ideas. If we talk about his religious beliefs, we can never agree. Mamma is the same. Just because they can't have a bit of fun, they don't allow me to either. I guess it's the fault of this stupid war. Everything I do seems to be wrong. It makes me feel so awkward. When I am on my own, I feel different, so I try to keep to myself. That doesn't really help because all I do is think about everything, and that gets me really fed up and frustrated.'

'I guess it's that old problem of the parent-child relationship,' I ventured. This was not really my scene at all. No training had prepared me for this! Here was a young girl going through the advanced stages of adolescence. This was not in any theological tomes I had read, and neither was it part of the syllabus in North Wales.

Inge simply ignored my comment and continued as though nothing had been said. 'Everything seems so extreme. I don't seem to be able to find—what do you call it?—the middle ground.'

'Or the happy medium,' I interjected.

'That's probably what I mean. All I manage to do is go round and round in circles. I don't seem to be going anywhere, and I wonder what is the point of anything. All my aims seem to be been dampened down by Papa, and my future seems to be dependent on his satisfaction with whatever I do. Seeing that we don't agree on this subject, I can't see myself doing much for my enjoyment. All I can think of is leaving home and leading an independent life. Is that ever going to happen? I don't seem to be going anywhere at the moment. The whole world can fall to pieces, for all I care.'

'I'm sure you don't mean that.'

'I can never say what I mean because I can never make things come out with the feeling I mean them to.'

'You are making a very good job of it. Your English is excellent.'

'I can't convey my feelings. It is so frustrating. I always seem so fake or overemotional. I have no confidence in what I say. I can never express things how I want to. I really want to get closer to people, but I never know if they want to or not. I never dare make the first move.'

A strong feeling welled up that by opening up in this way, Inge was getting very close to me. An inner voice prompted me to keep quiet.

'I want to know others, but do they want to know me? That's a stupid thing to say because if I go on at this rate, then I'm never going to find out. I suppose I'm scared of being rejected, really.'

At this point, I felt a distinct urge to put my arms around Inge and give her a big bear hug, but I felt this could be misconstrued, especially in the darkness. For better or for worse, I exercised great restraint.

'I just don't know what to do with myself. Everything I do is a failure. I don't get anywhere with anything, and I can't make people realise I really am trying. Why can't I do anything right for a change? I'm such a useless, complaining cow.'

'But you found me in the forest, and if it wasn't for you, I would be in the hands of the army,' I quickly interjected.

'I guess so,' she said, not sounding at all convinced. 'I just feel so useless and agitated, and I can't explain myself. I wish I knew English a bit better, and then maybe you would understand.'

I hastened to say that her English was excellent and she had no worries on that account, but she hardly seemed to notice what I had said. There was a long silence. I was at a complete loss for words. What could I say to this young girl who was coping with conflicting emotions and trying to come to terms with a host of new feelings?

After what seemed like an eternity and what sounded like sobs coming from Inge's direction, she simply said, 'Thank you for listening.'

She left me to my own thoughts. All I could hope for was that my listening had proved helpful to her. Very often, simply by articulating our feelings, things don't seem quite so bad. As the old adage has it, 'A problem shared is a problem halved.'

8

Language Difficulties

Walking and climbing all over Snowdonia was almost enjoyable. If we had been able to take out time and enjoy the views instead of going as fast as possible, we would have felt differently. As it was, there was a job to be done. Our fitness levels and stamina had to be increased, and there was no way round that. We were at war. No time for fun and games, although to be honest, we did have a good sing-song on some of our rambles—'Tramp up Snowdon with your woad on, never mind if you get rained or Snowdon', and the like. There had to be some light relief, otherwise life could get very heavy. Somebody once described laughing as internal jogging, and as such it was very good for one's health. I wouldn't want to disagree with that. God wants us to enjoy life and not have it taken away from us.

'The thief comes only to steal and kill and destroy. I came that they may have life, and have it abundantly' (John 10:10). I wonder what takes life away from us? Why do people do things that are deadening rather than life-giving? How many 'thieves' are there, waiting to steal our life-giving moments?

Whilst I pondered on the question, I heard a voice.

'Wie geht's dir, Heute?'

'Es geht mihr gut, danke.'

Whatever had happened during the day, this was how my day ended: with some German conversation. It always began with the same introduction. 'How are you today?' I managed the reply without any difficulty. 'I'm very well, thank you.' This was how I had to spend my evenings, getting to grips with the language. To say the least, my schoolboy German was very basic and stilted and did not prepare me for everyday conversation. What I needed was lots and lots of conversation to help me become more fluent and confident. No stone had been left unturned. My tutor had spent some time in Cologne before the war, so he knew some of the Kölnische dialect words. I simply had to assume that one day, this attention to detail would be useful, although at the time I had not been told where I was going in Germany or what my assignment was. Everything was on a need-to-know basis.

My progress was not very fast. Somehow, I just didn't click. Why does the German language need three words for *the*, not to mention all the different endings that *der, die,* and *das* have. *Complicated* is hardly a word that does justice to the matter. My tutor tried various methods, like reading an Agatha Christie whodunit in German, reading a German paper, or listening to German propaganda on the wireless. I was familiar with simple phrases: 'How are you?' 'Where do you come from?' 'What are you doing?' 'Where is the station?' However, putting more than one sentence together proved more difficult. Indeed, as I was later to discover, before you can put two sentences together, Germans always interrupt with their English. They are always highly motivated to improve their English.

Then my tutor had a sudden brain wave. 'You are a theological student, aren't you?'

I replied in the affirmative, wondering what could possibly be the cause of such a question.

'Well, then, why don't you improve your German by reading the psalms and the New Testament in German? If you know the Bible as well as you are supposed to, then I'm sure your language skills will come on by leaps and bounds.'

I didn't have a ready answer for this, but it did pass my mind that words like *crucifixion, resurrection, redemption, justification, circumcision,* and *atonement,* to name just a few, were not words in everyday parlance. However, nothing ventured, nothing gained. I promised to give it a try. To my complete surprise, my vocabulary did improve by leaps and bounds, as did my grammar and sentence construction. I also began to enjoy learning the language, and I gained confidence in being able to hold my own in a conversation. Whenever I had a spare moment, I tried to learn more vocabulary. Isn't it interesting how unlikely beginnings often turn out to be quite fruitful? The trick, it seems to me, is to keep an open mind. I think somebody once said that the closed mind is like a parachute: it doesn't work if it's not open. The closed mind is very boring and quite deadening. My life in Germany was to prove far from boring—and, thank goodness, my parachute did open!

9

Action Stations

The door opened slowly, and behind the torch I could just discern the figure of Karl. Behind him, I could just make out three more figures. Karl switched on the light. Imagine my utter disbelief when I saw the three people were none other than tall and lean Barrett, hairy Henry, and steady Spencer. I was speechless. Nothing could have prepared me for this. What in heaven's name were they doing here?

Before I could manage to form a few words, Karl spoke. 'Your friends arrived this evening.'

Apparently, it was the middle of the night. I had lost all sense of time.

'They came down the Rhine from the Dutch coast, hidden on a barge. I must leave you now, otherwise people will get suspicious. The Gestapo have left the village, but please be as quiet as possible. No doubt you will have a lot to talk about.'

That was an understatement if ever there was one. The excitement was so great that we all tried to speak at once. Eventually, some order returned, and I discovered that the three of them had been dropped off the Dutch coast by a submarine and had then made their way up the Rhine estuary in three inflatable canoes. It had been a very perilous journey until they were able to board a waiting barge carrying a cargo into southern Germany. Quite how they had managed to get through the coastal defences will forever remain a mystery; all they could say was that they were very fortunate. The weather was very wet and misty, and all the guards seemed to be distracted by air raids that had obviously been timed for their benefit.

'This is all very well,' I said, 'but why are you here?'

Henry, the extrovert, was the first to speak. 'After you left us at Bryn, we had a visit from the secret service telling us we had been chosen for an operation in Germany.'

Barrett chimed in. 'Why we were chosen, we have no idea, except our obvious association with you.'

'I guess they thought we all got on so well together that, we would make an excellent team,' interjected Spencer.

'Yes,' I interrupted, beginning to feel quite frustrated. 'But what is the purpose of your mission? I don't even why I am here.'

Barrett replied, 'As you rightly say, you have not been told why you are here. You were simply instructed to be dropped near to Cologne, where you would be picked up by the resistance. For reasons of security, in case you were discovered by the German police or military, you'd have no idea what your mission was.'

'All you realised was that you were very useful because of your fluency in German,' said Henry.

I blanched at the thought. My German was passable, but it could hardly be said to be fluent. I was beginning to wish I had taken more time with my German in North Wales.

'So why am I here?' I asked eagerly.

Barrett replied, 'We have to cause as much disruption as possible to German lines of communication. The Allied forces have landed on the beaches of Normandy, and so the more trouble we can cause behind German lines, the better it will be for our forces.'

'Obviously', retorted Henry

'And,' interjected Spencer, 'we have brought a quantity of explosives with us. We hope more will be given to us by the local resistance group.'

They all seemed quite happy with their task. I was less enamoured.

'Yes, but what's the plan?' I enquired, beginning to feel quite frustrated.

'That, my boy, is all down to you,' exclaimed Henry, as though that was the be-all and end-all of the matter.

To say the least, I was a bit taken aback. All this came as news to me. I certainly did not have any kind of plan in mind at all. After eventually collecting my thoughts, I said, 'Clearly we can't remain holed up in this convent indefinitely. Somebody is bound to discover us before long. In any case, a war is being waged, and we have an important part to play.'

I felt pleased I had said something that sounded important and relevant, but Henry very quickly brought me down to earth.

'So what is the plan, then?' he said, putting me on the spot.

Thinking on my feet, I replied, 'We will need to reconnoitre the city of Cologne before we can hatch a definite plan.'

'Yes, but how do we get into the city from this small village without drawing attention to ourselves?' Henry was beginning to irritate me with his questions.

'That's right,' agreed Spencer. 'Four young men would easily arouse suspicion and raise the question, "Why aren't they fighting for the homeland?" We might get away with it if we travelled alone.'

'I know!' said Henry. 'We could be wounded soldiers sent home from the front.'

At this point, to my relief, Barret came to my aid.

'You are forgetting one thing. The papers we have been given don't say we are soldiers. They say we are a Swiss family travelling home, after staying with some relatives in Cologne.'

For this to succeed, Henry had to be dressed as a mother, Barrett was the father, and Spencer and I were their two sons. All this had been decided in London long before I knew anything about it. I studied the papers in disbelief. It was true. All had been decided without my knowledge. My three colleagues had even brought some appropriate clothes and make-up with them.

Spencer and I were dressed in leather trousers (*leder hosen*) so typical of Swiss menfolk. Barrett was attired likewise, but he had something to rub into his hair to make him look older, and he was also growing a beard. I had wondered about that when I first saw him, and now I knew. Henry was the problem. However, he was small in stature, and he had curly hair which had been allowed to grow long. It was easy to tie a ribbon in it. Once he was in a skirt and blouse (filled out a little in the appropriate places), he looked very female. We had a good laugh at his expense. There were two caveats. His legs needed long stockings because they were very hairy, and he mustn't speak because his voice would immediately give away the game.

'Don't worry, Henry,' I said. 'If someone speaks to you, I shall simply say in my faultless German that you have had a stroke, and your speech has been affected.'

I should also say that our names had all been changed. We were now the Bloch family from Geneva: Arthur and Claudia with their two sons, Fritz and Roger. To be supposedly coming from Switzerland was a great advantage to me because it meant that my German could be Swiss German, and therefore excuses could be made. Again, attention had been given to detail. Remarkable. The secret service was continuing to rise in my estimation.

We still had the problem of actually getting into Cologne. It quickly became apparent we needed the help of Karl if we were to get anywhere with our discussion. We needn't have worried because Karl had it all wrapped up. Not for nothing are Germans noted for their efficiency. He came in a couple of hours and shared the news. We were to travel with him early in the morning in a horse-drawn cart which was generally used for carrying bales of hay. Because we were coming in from the country, this would not arouse any suspicion. Moreover, although Karl had an old car, petrol was extremely hard to come by. In fact, in that part of the world, most things were hard to come by.

As the sun rose, we slowly approached the Rhine and could see across the river, including the devastation that had been wrought by Allied bombs. The city had been almost flattened; very few buildings were left standing. There was rubble everywhere. The famous cathedral had also suffered damage. The twin spires gave an obvious navigation guide to allied aircraft. The spires, however, still stood, proudly reaching up to the sky. One of my learned friends—I've forgotten which one—informed me that the cathedral foundations were laid in 1248, but for a whole host of reasons, the building wasn't completed until 1880. I have often wondered what it was that stirred so many people to build such a magnificent structure when they were embroiled in abject poverty.

'Being a theology student,' whispered Barret, 'I suppose you know the cathedral is supposed to house the remains of the three wise men who visited Jesus at the time of his birth in Bethlehem.'

The situation did not allow for any discussion on the subject, but my inbred scepticism briefly raised a few questions. How did anyone know for sure the bones were those of the wise men? How did they know there were three wise men when the New Testament didn't specify how many there were? How did their bones find their way to this cathedral all the way from first-century Palestine? If Henry had been privy to these thoughts, he would no doubt have been sceptical enough to ask whether the wise men actually existed, but that was another matter altogether. No doubt some church historian or biblical scholar had some feasible answers to my questions, but for the moment, there were other, more pressing questions—not the least of which was how were we to get any farther than the small market that was taking place near to the Rhine. The place was crawling with police and soldiers. The Rhine bank itself was covered in barbed wire, and we could freely see that the two bridges in view were patrolled by soldiers. Our task of disrupting anything or anybody was not going to be a pushover.

As unobtrusively as possible, we surveyed the scene, and then the inevitable happened.

'Was machen Sie hier?' a policeman asked.

Without a second thought, I replied, 'Wir kaufen gemüse für meine Familie.'

It seemed a fair enough answer to me. After all, we were in the market, so to be buying vegetables seemed a logical thing to be doing. Thankfully, the policeman was easily satisfied, and we all breathed a big sigh of relief.

We hadn't gone very far when we were again interrupted. 'Ihre Papier, bitte.'

Without hesitation, we handed over our papers and hoped they would be seen as authentic. This time Karl was able to do the talking and explained that we were a Swiss family staying in his village, and he had given us a ride into the market. The explanation seemed to satisfy the soldier, but this was an important lesson for us. We really had to be on our guard, and it was probably better to not be around in the daytime at all. The trouble was that a curfew was in operation from 7 p.m. to 7 a.m., and that provided another host of difficulties. Simply getting from A to B in the dark without being stopped and interrogated was going to be a major problem. Having bought a few victuals from the meagre selection on offer, we rode home in the cart to decide on a plan of action. Needless to say, the ride was very bumpy, but amazingly we made the journey in about an hour without being stopped on the way. Somebody seemed to be on our side. Was it God? I discovered later that God was also on the side of the Germans! On soldiers' belts were inscribed the words 'Gott mit uns'—God with us. *Whose side is God on? Where do these questions keep coming from?* Later that evening, when we eventually arrived back at our hideaway, a discussion took place. For Henry, there wasn't a problem.

'There is no God because if there was, he would surely have stopped this war.' That was Henry's view, and he stated it very emphatically.

Barrett was more hesitant. 'I think there may be a God, but he isn't going to do things for us that we can easily do for ourselves.'

Spencer and I were of the same opinion, although we were happy to ask the questions and leave the answers open. We simply didn't know many of the answers, but we kept exploring, and we had the faith to explore the mystery we called God.

At this point, Henry became very irritated. 'This is all very well, having esoteric, theological discussions, but we are at war. Not only that, but we have a mission to fulfil, and we haven't got very far as yet.'

This brought us all to the matter in hand. After much discussion, we made a decision. I and Inge should go out as a couple and take a more detailed reconnaissance of Cologne. I was chosen because of my knowledge of German. Inge had yet to be asked.

10

A Romantic Assignment

'I will do anything you ask,' Inge replied enthusiastically. She was nothing if not adventurous—anything to get away from her parents, even if it was dangerous. 'But what precisely do you want me to do?'

'Malcolm is going to be your boyfriend, visiting you from Switzerland. You are going to be yourself.'

I detected a slight colouring in Inge's cheeks at the thought of being my girlfriend. I have to admit that my heart beat a little quicker. Was I afraid of the impending foray into the city, or was I excited at the prospect of walking out with Inge?

'Yes,' interjected Spencer. 'All we want you to do is have good look at one of the bridges over the Rhine.'

Henry chimed in. 'We are going to blow the bridge to smithereens. Hopefully this will cause massive disruption to the German communications.'

'What are smithereens?' Inge inquired

'I guess you could say very small pieces,' explained Spencer in his usual droll voice.

'We suggest that you go on the horse-drawn cart for a little of the way and then walk from there,' Barrett informed her. 'We think in this way, little attention will be drawn to you. A young couple out for a walk will not look suspicious.'

Off we went, hand in hand, supposedly like any carefree couple. I have to say that Inge enjoyed this more than I was. Maybe she simply didn't appreciate the dangers of being caught. She was soon to realise how difficult our mission was.

We managed to avoid a couple of roadblocks by sticking to paths through fields. Inge knew her way around, and for that I was very thankful. A farmer greeted us, but we simply waved and carried on. It was not advisable to get into any long conversations, even if we thought the person was friendly. One never knew who could be trusted in a time of war. The whole situation was completely surreal. A few hours ago, Inge had been sharing her intimate feelings with me, and now here I was behind enemy lines, walking hand in hand with her as though I hadn't a care in the world. You couldn't make it up. This was actually happening. In case of any eavesdroppers, any conversation we had was carried out in German. Naturally, Inge did most of the talking. She more or less carried on where she had left off a few hours previously. This time it I had to really concentrate in order to understand what she was saying.

The gist of her conversation was much the same as before. There had been another row with her parents. Apparently, her room had been left in an untidy state. If you ask me, she was being a typical young person, but her parents didn't see it that way. As far as they were concerned, bedrooms needed to be kept neat and tidy. Inge was beginning to feel very claustrophobic. In fact, she said precisely that.

'Ich kriege Platzangst.'

Then she went into a long diatribe of how awful she felt and that nobody understood her. She felt trapped and wanted to escape and get on with her own life.

Suddenly, the conversations came to an abrupt halt. 'Was machen Sie dann hier?' came a loud stentorian voice across the field.

'Wir besuchen meine Verwandten,' Inge shouted back. We were visiting relations. Why not?

The policeman came nearer and asked where our relations lived.

'Am Ubierring, in der Nähe von Chlodwigplatz,' replied Inge.

'Passen Sie gut auf. Soldaten sind überall.'

We thanked the policeman for his advice to take care and went on our way. Soldiers apparently were all over the place, so we had to be very careful. Quite what the policeman was doing in the farm we had just passed was not our business. Conversation ground to a halt. Even Inge realised the seriousness of our situation. We were on constant lookout. By this time, we were amongst the outskirts of Cologne. Devastation was everywhere. There were heaps of rubble and buildings shattered by Allied bombs.

A few citizens wandered about very slowly as though in a complete daze. Possibly they had lost all they owned as well as their families. I wondered how anyone could still be living amidst such chaos. Amazingly, a few shops were still standing, and the roads and tramlines were still visible.

Suddenly Inge whispered, 'Gib mir ein Küβchen, schnell.'

Without any further thought, I quickly gave her a peck on her cheek. To say I was surprised would be an understatement, but then all became clear. Out of the corner of my eye, I could see the hated Gestapo coming in our direction. Why did they always wear those black leather jackets? Taking my cue from Inge, I decided there and then to take the kissing a step further. We kissed on the lips—a very long, lingering kiss. This was something new! I had kissed a few English girls in my time, mainly just for fun, but here I was kissing a young German girl. The sap began to rise because I could feel her body hard against mine. It was so enjoyable that I almost forgot the gravity of our situation.

As luck would have it, the Gestapo simply thought we were a pair of young lovers and laughed at us. 'Guck mal Da! Zwei junge lieben Vögeln. Gehen Sie weiter. Beeilen sich.'

He obviously thought we were two young lovebirds. We didn't argue the point but did as he commanded and hurried along as quickly as possible. Luck was on our side, but how long would it last? With no more interruptions, we arrived at our destination, the Deutzer Brücke. The bridge crossed over the Rhine and connected the city centre with the Cologne suburb, Deutz. Inge, corrected me by saying that since 1935, the bridge had been renamed the Hindenburgh Bridge after the second German president, who had died in 1934. I could clearly see that for some strange reason, the bridge was only guarded at the city side; our side was free of guards. Trams, traffic such as there were, and pedestrians were free to go over to the other side. I could also clearly see that the bridge was a suspension bridge, using chains securely anchored to the bank.

My immediate thought was that if we could plant sufficient explosives under these anchors, the bridge would collapse under its own weight. Armed with this information, we decided to board a tram and make our way back to the village. Going by tram seemed less arduous than going on foot. We could only go so far by tram, and then we had to walk the final two or three kilometres. We reached the village without any further alarms. Unfortunately, there were no further kisses.

On arriving back at the house, we were greeting by Ursula. 'My husband, Karl, has been taken by the SS and will probably be tortured.'

This was devastating news.

'Why on earth has he been taken?' I asked.

'Because he insisted on giving the last rites to some people in the next village. They were thought to belong to the resistance and were about to be put before a firing squad.'

She went on to explain that all pastors, be they Catholic or Protestant, were carefully watched by the authorities. Increasing religious objections to Nazi policies led the Gestapo to carefully monitor church organisations. The Nazi regime sought to suppress any source of ideology other than its own, and it set out to muzzle or crush the churches in the so-called *Kirchenkampf*. When Church leaders voiced their misgiving about the euthanasia programme and Nazi racial policies, Hitler intimated that he considered them 'traitors to the people' and went so far as to call them 'destroyers of Germany'. The extreme anti-Semitism prompted some Christians to outright resistance. Some pastors, we were told, had paid for their opposition with their lives.

Ursula related all this to us in hushed tones. She was obviously very distressed and told us the news with a tear-stained face. How does one cope when one's beloved partner has been captured and will, in all probability, undergo torture? Clearly, our lives were in greater danger than we'd thought. If the SS had been in the next village, what were our chances of remaining hidden?

We needn't have worried; Ursula had everything in hand. The Germans used to say of their Hausfrau, 'Kinder, kuche, kirche.' In other words, the woman's work was to bring up the children, feed them, and make sure they attended church. Ursula had other gifts, not the least of which was helping us to make plans. She was an organiser par excellence.

Ursula had decided we would have to move again. In any case, to stay too long in the same place simply courted danger. What we hadn't realised was that Ursula owned a shop in the city where she carried out her watch repairs. She travelled into the city every day by horse and cart. She was such a familiar figure that it was thought nobody would think of stopping her and asking where she was going. We were to travel on two successive days in two groups. Our hiding place was to be inside the casing of two grandfather clocks. As it happened, the shop had remained untouched by Allied bombs, and Ursula thought we could hide in the basement where she had her workshop. I was to travel with big Barrett in the morning; Spencer and Henry were to follow the next day.

In the morning, I dutifully expressed my thanks to the nuns and hoped they had not been too inconvenienced. If we had ever been discovered, it would have been curtains for them. Some people are naturally good and will do anything for their fellow human beings, even if it endangers their own lives. This principle of altruism is very hard to account for by any scientific theory. How refreshing to come across people who are not ego driven but completely selfless.

It was still dark as Barrett and I scrambled into the cart and into the clocks. Although the clocks were large enough to stand in (unless one was as tall as Barrett), there was a tendency for bits of metal to protrude into your body when the cart gave a jolt. We had to resist the temptation to cry out with the shock of the impact. I briefly made out in the dim light that the cart was being driven not by Ursula but by a young man. This, I later discovered, was one of the sons, Norbert. Apparently, this was a normal occurrence, and it was vital not to do things out of the ordinary. Norbert attended a school in the city, and this was part of his daily routine. I hadn't noticed him, but the other son, Gustav, was also travelling with us. My concern was that if too many people knew of our whereabouts, then it was only a matter of time before we were discovered. I need not have worried. The boys were completely trustworthy.

The clocks were clearly on view for all to see, but sometimes the obvious could be overlooked. I was reminded of the old story about an elderly Arab who regularly crossed over the border from Israel into Egypt. The border guards always searched his donkey and cart for contraband but never found anything. Some years later, a guard came across the old man and asked him if he'd ever managed to smuggle anything into Egypt. 'Yes, I did,' came the reply. 'I was smuggling donkeys.'

I knew we were getting close to our destination when I heard the occasional tram rumble past. There was one guard post where we had to stop, and papers were asked for, but before Ursula could find them, she was waved on. The plan had worked! She was such a familiar figure that no questions were asked. And so it was that we arrived in one piece at the watch and jewellery shop in the Ubierring. Spencer and Henry arrived the following day, also without incident. In addition, the explosives they had brought over from England were also transported. Was God really on our side?

11

Explosive Outcomes

I had now been in Cologne for a week, my friends for four days—and we had done nothing at all that could hinder the German war effort. We felt very frustrated. We needed to do something, and fast. Conveniently, whilst working at her clocks and watches, Ursula could assist us in our plans. She was not backwards in coming forward if anything didn't seem right. The plan was that we should attempt to blow up the entrance to the Deutzer Bridge, and this should take place the day after the full moon, in two days. This gave us sufficient time to get ourselves organised. The main problem was simply moving around the city after 7 p.m. when there was a curfew. Public transport was clearly out of the question, and simply walking the three miles to the bridge with explosives would not be feasible. Soldiers were constantly on the lookout.

We were completely stumped, but then Ursula came up with the idea of an ambulance. These were often seen during the curfew, especially during an air raid. A message was sent back to England asking that a small air raid take place in two days in a suburb of Cologne. Yes, I know you, dear reader, want to ask how we sent the message back to England. Ursula knew someone in the German resistance who had a short-wave radio. It was amazing what the resistance people had and what they did. The air raid was to be not only a distraction but also a reason for ambulances to be on the move in the city. Ursula knew one of the drivers could be trusted, and she arranged for him to stop in a quiet place so we could jump in, hopefully unseen. This meant we had to make our way to the pick-up spot before curfew.

Ursula had done her homework. The ambulance was to pick us up in the grounds of a hospital. Where else? All we had to do was get there unnoticed. For obvious reasons, we travelled alone and by different routes. If we were captured and interrogated, then we did not know the whereabouts of anyone else, and who was to say that we weren't lone wolves? I travelled by tram because it was thought I might need to use some German, if only to say *Guten tag*. An old bicycle was found for Henry, and the other two walked the three miles to the hospital. Ursula had given us precise directions, so nothing could go wrong—could it?

When you are trying to look inconspicuous, you easily get the feeling that everybody is looking at you. In order to look normal, and for something to hide behind, I bought a local newspaper, the *Kölner Stadt-Anzeiger*. Under normal circumstances, this would have provided plenty of reading material, but now there was very little to read. Suffice it to say, the paper served my purpose. I kept to myself and was undisturbed, even when police boarded the tram. As planned, I left the tram in the vicinity of St Elisabeth Krankenhaus in the Cologne suburb of Lindenthal. Near the hospital was some property which had been almost flattened by bombs, but part of it could be entered, and it was there I was to meet my three comrades.

I was first to arrive, and Barrett and Spencer arrived sometime later, but where was Henry? Darkness was fast approaching, as was the curfew. Where was he? What had happened to him?

'Where is Henry?' Barrett inquired.

'Oh, he'll turn up. He always does,' muttered Spencer. 'A bad penny always turns up.'

'I don't think he is a bad penny in any shape or form. In any case, I am getting quite anxious. We can't be a man down at this early stage in our operation. If he has been captured, he might give away our whole operation. The security forces will definitely be on the alert.'

'Very true,' agreed Spencer.

'There's absolutely nothing we can do now, so let's keep quiet and try to get some sleep.'

As ever, Ursula had the foresight to provide us with some iron rations and water, just in case. There was nothing for it but to make ourselves as comfortable as possible in the derelict building—or what remained of it—and wait for the morning.

Dawn broke, and with it some warmth. The autumnal night had been none too warm. Our predicament now was that we didn't know what to do. Should we somehow make our way back to Ubierring, or stay put? While we were debating the issue, to our surprise and delight, Henry turned up. It transpired that soon after setting off the day before, his front tyre had punctured. There was no way he could carry on. He decided, for better or for worse, to return to base. Ursula somehow passed a message, via a resistance member, to the ambulance driver to tell him that the operation had been delayed by one day. Not only that, but just in the nick of time, the planned air raid had been aborted. In the meantime, the puncture was repaired, and Henry arrived without further mishap. There were sighs of relief all round. He had also brought more victuals, the usual black bread and some *würst*. I wasn't too keen on sausage, but under those circumstances, I was prepared to eat anything. Happily, he also brought some *apfelsaft* to wash it all down. What a treat—real apple juice!

We dozed in the afternoon, and dusk soon appeared. One by one, under cover of darkness, we dodged our way through the devastation to the hospital. Was it a miracle that bombs had left it more or less unscathed—or was this the precision bombing of the Allies? The ambulance was parked amongst other ambulances, as planned, but ours had a distinctive scratch on its rear doors. We quickly jumped in without being seen, and as we did so, we heard distant bombing. The air raid had started bang on time. The plan was that Spencer and Henry should be wrapped up in bloodied bandages whilst Barrett and I donned white coats. Should we be stopped, it looked as though two doctors were tending two patients who had been injured in the air raid.

We hadn't gone far when we were stopped. A wailing siren was the precursor to the back door being opened. A burly policeman looked in and quickly got the picture. 'Du liebe Zeit. Beilen sich.' Our ruse had paid off. He took one look at the two 'patients' and told us to make haste. This our driver did, all the way to the Eduardus Krankhaus, which was situated in the suburb of Deutz, very close to the bridge. So far, so good, but now came the real challenge: how to approach the bridge undetected.

The only thing in our favour was the blackness of the night. There were no street lights because of the blackout, and the buildings still standing were also in total darkness for the same reason. Consequently, we could hardly see our hands in front of our faces. We decided to stay together for the simple reason that if we separated, there was every chance we would not meet up again. I led the way because I had been the one who had reconnoitred the bridge a few days previously. Luckily, I had the sort of brain that made a mental map of places, and so I felt fairly confident that we would find the bridge.

After making very slow progress and dodging into doorways if we thought we heard any kind of noise, the bridge came into view. As previously mentioned, the guard post was at the opposite end of the bridge. Two guards would regularly patrol the bridge from one end to the other. It took them ten minutes to get from our end of the bridge, the Deutz end, to the city end and then back again. In other words, we had less than ten minutes to get ourselves in place under the bridge. As the guards approached, we would be visible if we took longer. Once in place, we would wait for twenty minutes so that we could catch our breath and be ready to place the explosives under the bridge stanchions. If the timers were set for an hour, this would give us time to make our escape before all hell broke loose.

Believe it or not, everything went smoothly. The guards were very predictable, and their actions could be timed to the second. This was one of the times when German efficiency worked to our advantage. Not a word was spoken; we all knew what we had to do. Having set the charges—which incidentally, we had carried around our bodies as though we were on a suicide mission—we quietly made our way down to the river. Slowly and without a sound, we slipped into the Rhine. To say it was cold would be an understatement. The icy water seemed to penetrate deep into our bodies. In addition, we had to avoid the odd bits of debris floating about. Some of the objects were quite large.

We carried out our plan without a word. In order to get back to Ubierring as quickly as possible, we had to swim across the river but also upstream—against the current. We knew this was possible to do because Karl had told us he had done it many times as a young lad. The Rhine had quite a strong flow, but this was where all our endurance training came in. I had wondered what it had all been for, climbing in Snowdonia and swimming in the cold sea of Penmaenmawr. Now I knew. The river temperature made our swim doubly difficult, and we reached the other side breathless, but there was no time to lose. We had to make ground as quickly as possible before the explosives did their job.

From the riverbank, back to our base was a fairly short walk under normal circumstances. However, I have no recollection whatsoever of how we completed the distance. All I know is the adrenalin continued to flow, and I dimly recall a massive explosion somewhere in the distance. We had done our job. Still soaked through and totally exhausted, we reached the shop without being stopped by anyone. One reason could be there were fewer military personnel around than usual because many had been posted to the front to try to thwart the advance of the Allies who had landed in Normandy. As one might expect, Ursula was ready and waiting. She opened the door just sufficiently for us to squeeze through and then quickly shut it. We were back at base.

12

A Bridge Too Far?

It goes without saying that Cologne was now a city in turmoil. There was a picture of the bridge in the local press. The stanchions had been wrenched from their moorings, and the whole structure was hanging by a thread. It didn't actually fall into the river, but clearly it was no longer traversable by traffic or by people. Who had caused the explosion? Where could the perpetrators be? How had they escaped detection? Would there be more trouble in the future? Was anybody harbouring these people? If so, and they were caught, the posters said, there would be immediate execution. No wonder Ursula was worried. Not only was her husband in prison, but she was continuing to harbour four Englishman. What could we do? Our only option was to stay where we were. The dangers of moving around were obvious. We hoped the routine of Ursula, which she continued without fail, would not cause any suspicion.

The problem was that after a week cooped up in the cellar, we got cabin fever.

'I'm fed up of being in here,' Henry blurted out one morning. 'I need some fresh air.'

'Just be patient,' murmured Spencer. 'Nothing lasts forever.'

'It's all very well saying that, but how long are we going to hang about doing nothing?' retorted Henry.

Our frustrations were coming to the surface, and the situation was becoming more intense by the minute. There was relief all round when Inge made a surprise appearance. She was very cheerful—and more good looking than ever.

'I've come to cheer you all up,' she said.

This may well have been true, but I had a sneaking suspicion she had really come to see me. She brought us up to date with all that was happening in the city and the prospects for our future escape. Furthermore, a note had been secretly sent out of the prison to say that her papa was still alive; one of the guards appeared to be anti-Nazi. Even in the midst of horror and terrible privation, it was good to know there was still a modicum of humanity. This was good news indeed, but there was more.

'The Allies have landed in Normandy and are slowly moving into France,' Inge said.

'Yippee!' shouted Henry.

How she found out this information, I could only guess. Presumably a member of the resistance had a short-wave radio and was able to listen in to the BBC.

'That is very, very good news,' Barrett quietly said. 'But given this information, I think it is incumbent upon us to try some more disruption of enemy communication systems.'

'I agree entirely,' I said. 'There is a railway bridge going over the Rhine, and even better, it isn't far from here. Surely we could cause some disturbance to the railway system. What a big impact that would have on the German economy.'

'I think you are talking about the Süd Bridge,' Inge said. 'For some reason, Allied bombs have not touched this bridge but the other, bigger railway bridge, the Hohenzollern, has been very badly damaged.'

'I think this may well be a bridge too far,' droned Spencer.

As soon as Ursula appeared from the shop upstairs, we told her our intentions.

'Machen Sie Spass,' she said earnestly.

'No, we are not joking,' I quietly replied.

Ursula was clearly none too pleased with our plan. 'There is a lot of unrest in the city. People are finding it difficult to move around without be stopped, searched, and asked for papers,' she explained.

'We really would like to do this,' Barrett said. 'It is essential that we do our best to disrupt German lines of communication. That is why we are here. Moreover, I promise you that after this operation we will not return here.'

This final promise seemed to win over Ursula. There was a look of sheer relief on her face. The tension of having four Englishman locked up in her cellar was beginning to tell.

'There is a small problem,' Spencer interjected. 'The explosives we brought with us have all been used. We need to get some more from somewhere.'

'Leave it to me,' replied Ursula, and she left us to go back to her work upstairs.

It took Ursula three days to bring some explosives. She had brought them into the city on her cart amply covered by a supply of potatoes, onions, and carrots that had just been harvested by a farmer near Kleineichen. That seemed to be the easy part. What was our plan of campaign to be? At least this gave us something constructive to put our minds to. Fortunately, I had found a few German books to read. Barrett tried to keep a journal of all our experiences. Spencer, being a mathematician, whiled away the hours counting the number of trams every hour. He even managed to work out their rates of acceleration. He calculated all this just from listening. I began to wonder what we could discover if we spent more time just listening to God. Most of our time in prayer is spent in us telling the Almighty what to do. As if he doesn't know! Prayer is surely about God telling us what to do, and that demands a great deal of listening.

Henry, on the other hand, was a scientist. He had to be up and doing, and this enforced imprisonment was anathema to him. The thought of actually leaving came as a great relief to him. I had a feeling that his scientific education prevented Henry from making a leap of faith into Christianity. In fact, he said as much.

'I am only interested in facts—what can be observed and experimented on. How can you believe in something that you can't see?' I heard him say.

'You can't see love,' I said, 'only the effects of love. And how can science describe beauty? Or, indeed, can science tell us why we are here? Scientists may, in the course of time, tell us how we came to exist on this planet but not why we are here. Warming to my theme, I also said, 'The wonders of scientific discovery simply highlight what a magnificent world has been created by God. Furthermore, my faith is not a leap in the dark but based on trust. A trapeze artist flying through the air has to trust that her partner hanging from the other trapeze will be there to catch her. We know about trust because that is what we learned from each other in our training. Trust is a learned experience. You don't learn to swim by sitting on the side of the swimming pool.'

This was quite a long speech from me, but it kept Henry quiet for a little while. There were more urgent matters pressing on our minds.

'I'm not entirely sure how this mission is going to be accomplished,' pronounced Barrett.

'I think that before we decide anything, there should be a careful reconnaissance of the bridge, as we did last time,' said Henry.

'I agree,' said Spencer. 'It would be foolhardy to undertake this plan without some prior knowledge.'

As one might guess, the task fell to me, and again we decided that I should go with Inge. I could not disagree with this suggestion at all. On the contrary, the thought of a walk with Inge, however dangerous, filled me with great enthusiasm. It might even mean that if things got especially tense, I could give her another big kiss. I couldn't wait.

Clearly, we had to go on our little excursion during the day. During the hours of the curfew, walking around would be out of the question. We would simply stroll to the Rhine, sit on one of the benches overlooking the river, and make our observations. To the casual observer, we would be an innocent, courting couple admiring the view. This could only take place at the weekend, when Inge wasn't attending her *Hochschule*. As planned, she came the next Saturday, but it poured with rain. Even courting couples don't sit out in the pouring rain to admire the view. However, the following day was ideal: not too sunny and a little haze in the air. We carried a Bible so it looked as though we were going to Church; this was, after all, a Sunday. We instinctively held hands and lingered as we walked through the local park, chatting in German in case we were overheard. Sometimes it seems as though, in war time, even trees have ears. Clearly, Inge felt the same way about me as I felt about her. We reached our destination unhindered and sat down on the first bench we saw. I put my arm round Inge and gazed at the view.

'Was haben wir hier?' a loud, powerful voice bellowed out.

I immediately jumped up out of my seat and tried to act as naturally as possible. I replied, 'Ich komme aus Kleineichen wo meinen Eltern wohnen. Ich habe ein paar Gemüse für meine kranken Oma mitgebracht. Inge, hier, ist meine Freudin und wir haben nur für eine Stunde getroffen.'

I hoped that by saying my grandma was ill and I was meeting my girlfriend just for an hour, I would attract a modicum of sympathy.

'Haben sie Papiere?'

Fortunately, Ursula had insisted we didn't go out without our papers. The soldier took our papers and paused. We waited expectantly. He gave us a long, bemused look and then with a sigh moved on. Lady Luck was on our side. As a mark of gratitude, I gave Inge a long, slow kiss. This seemed to me as good an excuse as any, and she didn't complain. Indeed, she was very compliant. War could have been a million miles away as we embraced on that river bench, but then our idyll was disturbed as a train rumbled over the bridge.

The bridge was well guarded on our side of the river, and there seemed to be no easy access. However, after resisting the temptation provided by Inge, I gazed at the bridge, and a plan slowly formed in my mind. It was pushing our luck to stay too long there, and so after about fifteen minutes, we returned to base.

I disclosed my plan to the other three. I explained that the bridge had a large, square support pillar about a hundred metres from the bank. If we could place our explosives there, then that would cause sufficient structural damage to make the bridge impassable.

'How on earth are we going to do that?' shouted the others in unison.

'Wouldn't it be better to simply blow up a train and cause chaos that way?' one of them offered.

Nothing could persuade me to take that approach. I was firmly against an action which could entail the loss of life.

'We've already been in the river and felt how freezing cold it is. How are we going to survive?' another asked.

A very reasonable objection, I thought. I replied, 'Isn't it possible to coat ourselves in some kind of fat to keep the cold out?' I also reminded them we were all good swimmers, so if we managed to enter the river south of the bridge and then gently move with the current under cover of some driftwood, we could steer a course towards the pillar. After uttering some misgivings the others agreed the plan had some merit. The truth was they couldn't think of anything better. Neither could I.

Another problem was that we would have to wait at least two more weeks if we wanted to move under cover of a new moon. Such a long wait was out of the question; none of us would survive. In any case, Ursula had heard that the security police were beginning to search a lot of the buildings that were still standing. Presumably, they had gotten wind of the resistance using short-wave radio, as well as rumours that some Englishmen were about to carry out more nefarious business. Things were getting urgent. In fairness to Ursula and her family, we needed to make a move pretty quickly. All we needed was some fat to rub on our bodies.

As usual, Ursula came up trumps. In spite of all the shortages, she managed to persuade her local butcher to part with some animal fat. This was melted down into a useable form and mixed with some soot from the fireplace. The result was a very black and smelly mixture. We assumed the smell would disappear once we were in the water. After daubing ourselves with this concoction, we said our heartfelt goodbyes to Ursula and Inge. If anybody could be described as a Christian, it would be Ursula. I discovered an interesting fact that in Germany, a Christian is translated as *ein Christ*. In other words, one doesn't simply try to imitate Christ—one has actually to try to become 'a Christ'. I spent many a long hour pondering over the implications of that. My farewell to Inge took a little longer. We embraced and had a long, lingering kiss. Thankfully, she ignored the greasy mess on my face. I wondered if I would ever see her again. The four of us took our leave under cover of darkness.

We left the house one by one, merged easily into the shadows, and we made our way to the river. As I have said, it is always dangerous to move about during the hours of the curfew, so we were doubly cautious. At the faintest sound, we froze and waited until the sound had dissipated.

Eventually, after what seemed a lifetime, we reached the river, downstream from the bridge. Thankfully, the moon was blanketed by thick cloud; we had difficulty seeing anything. All we heard was the gentle flow of the majestic Rhine, one of the longest rivers in Europe flowing all the way from the Swiss Alps. We found a little jetty that didn't have any boats moored alongside so we could easily slip into the murky depths of the river. We didn't have to wait long before some driftwood and a couple of branches floated along. This was our cover. Having recovered from the initial shock of the coldness of the water, we gently and silently paddled our way to the bridge. This was not difficult because we were flowing with the current.

After reaching the bridge, we crammed the explosives into some crevices between the stones. Through the ages, the force of the water had worked away and created these cracks. The explosives themselves had been carefully wrapped in waterproof material. The timers were affixed to the stone with strong tape. We worked quickly and silently. Each of us knew precisely what to do. The whole operation lasted no more than five minutes. Now we had to make our escape.

Our lords and masters back in England were very good at sending men and woman on perilous missions, but they never made plans for these people to return to England after the mission was accomplished. They were always left to their own devices for the return journey.

13

Afloat

We had endlessly discussed our means of escape. One possibility was to return the same way my three friends had arrived—that was, down the Rhine to Amsterdam. Another idea was to go up the Rhine into Switzerland and neutral territory. A variation of this was to go as far as Koblenz and then travel up the Moselle into France, where we would eventually meet Allied forces. After all, the news was that the Allies had landed in Normandy, and we assumed they were making progress in liberating France. Any form of transport other than a boat was discounted, especially because we wanted to stay together as a group; it was felt to be too dangerous.

After much argument, we decided that our best policy was to board a boat immediately after we set the explosives. Easier said than done! Where would the boat come from? Again our resistance friends came to the rescue. A narrow boat loaded with coal would be moored two hundred metres from the bridge. A dry set of clothes would also be there, plus some warm water with which to remove the fat from our bodies.

As we clambered onto the boat, the detonators did their work. A huge explosion rent asunder the stillness of the night. There was the sound of falling masonry and iron structures as they fell with a huge splash into the river below. The bridge had not been completely demolished, but it was obviously unsafe for a train to cross. As we savoured our success, a piercing light shot out across the water, and we found ourselves in its knife-like beam. We had been caught hook, line, and sinker.

There was no escape. In no time at all, four heavily armed soldiers appeared and directed us with their guns onto the river bank. There was no crew on the boat because of the curfew. We were unceremoniously shoved into the back of an army van, and off we drove. Although we were all elated at the success of our mission, there was apprehension, anxiety, and downright fear. Where we were going? What was going to happen? A firing squad? Torture? Solitary confinement? My mind raced through all sorts of dreadful possibilities. The four of us fell completely silent, each lost in his own thoughts. There was nothing to be said.

After a short time, we arrived at some kind of military headquarters on the outskirts of Cologne. Fortunately, we were allowed to shower because we smelt horrendously; the animal fat was still on our bodies and had begun to make its presence felt. Eventually, we were hauled in front of an imposing figure whom we took to be the commandant. If my German was correct, he informed us we would be travelling in the morning to another location, where the Gestapo would interrogate us. There could easily have followed a sleepless night, but I always kept in my mind what one of my tutors had taught me: the only reality was now. Indeed, if you believe in God, then God is only in the present moment. God is not in the past or the future, only in the now. Therefore Christians pray for sufficient strength to get through each day. 'Give us this day our daily bread.' When the children of Israel were miraculously given bread in the desert, it only lasted one day. If they tried to store it up, the bread went mouldy. With these thoughts, I managed to go to sleep, although I think my three companions found it more difficult.

Morning arrived. We were actually given some breakfast, such as it was: water and pumpernickel. We were soon jostled into the back of a van, and off we drove at the crack of dawn. After a short time, there was a terrific explosion—a bomb had dropped very near to us. We swerved, hit a big bump, and overturned. The door of the van had been badly buckled, and we wasted no time in forcing it open. The driver and his colleague had been thrown through the windscreen and were dead. We were free for the moment. Almost without thinking, we stripped the two Germans of their uniforms. Spencer and I were a similar size, so we put them on. We were now two German soldiers transporting two English spies. With a great effort of muscle and sheer willpower, we were able to right the van. Mercifully, it did not catch fire.

All around us was general pandemonium. Explosions continued, sirens sounded, and civilians ran hither and thither. The emergency services were very slow to come to the scene. Our actions had been totally unnoticed. The vehicle started immediately, and we drove off. Our instinct was to go back to plan A and board the boat that was our original intention. We just hoped that it was still in situ. The journey back through Cologne was hazardous, to say the least. There were ruins everywhere, and the roads were full of potholes. The emergency services and the police were in abundance but nobody stopped us. To all intents and purposes, we were inconspicuous. A German military vehicle was a common enough sight, and who would have the temerity to halt it and ask questions of the driver? No one did.

We arrived at our original point of departure, and to our enormous relief, the boat we had originally intended to escape on was still moored. My three companions slipped on board whilst I drove the van to a place where it could be left without anyone asking any questions. When we were all aboard, we persuaded the captain and his mate to set sail immediately so that we could travel some distance before the curfew came into operation. He didn't need much persuasion. To be caught with the four of us on board would have spelt disaster for him. The engine sprang into action, and we cast off and slowly made our way into the centre of the river, well away from any prying eyes on the banks. The four of us collapsed into some bunks in the cabin, exhausted. How long would this state of bliss last?

14

The Rhine

To say our position was precarious would be a massive understatement. It could not be long before the authorities discovered that four English terrorists were on the loose. The only thing in our favour was that the native Germans were beginning to get very nervous. Everyone was beginning to look to the west and think about the slowly advancing Allies. Be that as it may, we still needed to remain undetected. We had done our work, and now our sole objective was to get back to dear old Blighty.

For a few hours, we made slow progress towards Bonn. There was nothing of outstanding beauty in this part of the Rhine. In any case, we were travelling in the wee small hours, so we were encased in darkness. This part of the journey was uneventful, and as dusk approached, we found a quiet mooring on the outskirts of the city. Our cargo was coal, mined in the industrial heartland of Germany known as the *Ruhr Gebiet*. As we travelled, in the heart of all the coal, we fashioned a small place in which four bodies could hide should the need arise. This hiding place was impossible to detect from the outside; it was absolutely covered in piles of coal. Even a dog would never have been able to sniff us out. Little did I know how soon this would be put to use.

The next day saw us leave our moorings without any bother. This was an ordinary working barge—a very common sight on the river.

Who could possibly want to question our business? The four of us had to stay out of sight. If we spoke, it had to be in whispers. Water carries sound all too easily, and we didn't want any English floating across the water to attentive ears. If only we could stay on the deck to admire the view. This was a lovely part of the Rhine, the so-called Rhine gorge, covered with vineyards and ancient castles, and it was quite romantic. My thoughts wandered back to Inge. What was she doing now? Would I ever see her again? Would she ever be able to make peace with her parents?

We were travelling against the flow of the river, so our speed was quite ponderous. I can only say that we meandered down towards Koblenz. This is where the Moselle meets the Rhine at a place called three corners, *Dreiecke*. We reckoned if there was going to be any trouble, this would be as likely a place as any. To make doubly sure of our safety, the four of us crawled into our hiding place and bedded down for the night. Not a single word was spoken; we knew that our safety depended on absolute silence.

Then we heard the sound of jackboots on the deck. This was the last thing we wanted to hear—the sound of the German military. We hardly dared breathe, let alone move. The boots seemed to be around for a long time. We felt very vulnerable and scared because there was absolutely nothing we could do except wait. We were completely in the hands of other people—and in the hands of God. I wondered why it was that only in times of distress and crisis did people turn to God. All we could do was hope the ship's papers were in order and the captain would not give anything away. It was certainly in his interests to not betray our presence. All went eerily quiet. What had happened? Were we still being observed from afar, or were the police still on board? Was it safe to come out of hiding? How long had we been undercover? How long could we stay there?

Our unspoken questions, and our prayers, were answered when we heard the engine spring into life. Our imprisonment came to an end when the captain started removing some of the coal to allow us to come out. It transpired that the military had indeed been on board and given the boat a thorough search. They had not said who or what they were looking for, but the captain and his mate had been thoroughly questioned. Where were they from? Where were they going? Who were they working for? Had they any papers? Happily, the police seemed satisfied that everything was in order. We continued on our journey.

I have deliberately not said anything about our captain simply because we knew nothing about him at all, not even his name. In times of war, everything is on a need-to-know basis, and we didn't need to know anything about him. We were entirely in his hands in a position of great trust. His primary objective was to deliver the coal to the markets of Switzerland. Nothing could prevent him from fulfilling his duty, certainly not any additional human cargo.

Again, I was sorry we couldn't stay on deck to admire and take in the views presented by the Rhine Gorge and the Drachenfels. All we could do was keep out of sight and wonder what was round the corner. We didn't have long to wait. A river police launch was hot on our tails. The sound of a powerful engine danced across the river and warned us of approaching danger. As quick as lightning, we clambered into our hiding place and again held our breath. This time our luck ran out. The police must have had their suspicions aroused on their first visit because this time they brought dogs with them. Dogs are very good at sniffing, and in no time at all they had detected our hiding place. We were caught red-handed. Without ceremony, we were manhandled onto the police launch, and away we sped. What happened to the captain and his mate, I have never been able to discover. Of course, we told the police they were entirely innocent, and we had hidden ourselves without their knowledge.

15

Incarceration

The only words that can describe my feelings at this point are utter and complete desolation. I felt totally empty, devoid of any shred of comfort. There wasn't even the presence of my companions to offer mutual support and relief. A little conversation would have been a great help. We had been separated and placed in separate cells. At least, I assumed my friends had been placed in a cell and had not come to an untimely death. My cell was furnished with a mattress on the floor and a bucket. That was it. A small shaft of light found its way through a tiny window high above my bed. There was no way I could look out onto the world. My future looked pretty hopeless.

After an indeterminate length of time, a slit was formed in the door, and a mug of liquid was pushed through. I can only say with certainty that the mug contained liquid. There was no taste whatsoever. For all I knew, I could have been poisoned. Anything seemed possible in that black hole.

By the following morning some light came into the cell, and my eyes had become accustomed to the dim light—not that there was anything to see. In the distance, I could hear shrieks and screams and wondered when my turn would come. I began to daydream and wondered just what it was in men—and it was usually men—that made them want to inflict so much suffering on their fellow human beings. Do they derive some kind of gratification from watching others writhe in pain? Do they feel powerful as they take advantage of the vulnerability of those they have captured?

I began to think of the injunction of Jesus: 'If someone strikes you on the right cheek, turn to him the other also … love your enemies and pray for those who persecute you' (Matthew 5:30, 44). Not exactly the words I wanted to recall at that precise moment, yet what else could I do? Becoming violent in my situation would not only achieve nothing but was also impossible. As I wrestled with these texts, another one came to mind: 'My grace is sufficient for you, for my power is made perfect in weakness … that is why, for Christ's sake, I delight in weaknesses, in insults, in hardships, in persecutions, in difficulties. For when I am weak, then I am strong' (2 Corinthians 12:9–10).

All very well for St Paul, I thought. *He was a saint, but I am an ordinary mortal who finds such sentiments extremely difficult to put into practice. To actually delight in hardships, and the like, sounds a bit too much for my liking.* All I wanted at that moment was a decent meal and my own comfortable bed to relax into. Yet there is something about being in extremity that elicits the realisation we can't do everything under our own steam. To rely solely on ourselves is a recipe for disaster. Actually, when we are weak, then we realise our dependence on God, and it is that realisation which brings us strength. Interestingly, Paul's beautiful letter to the church at Philippi was written whilst he was in prison, and *The Pilgrim's Progress* was written whilst Bunyan was imprisoned.

I have no idea how long these ideas were circulating round my brain. My thoughts were rudely interrupted by guards opening the door and roughly handling me down the dark corridor. What was going to be my fate? A firing squad? Thumb screws? Beating? Electric shock? What horrific torture had my captors devised? I was roughly dumped in a very hard chair, bound and blindfolded. I held my breath and waited, fearing the worst. There wasn't a sound. This was the silent treatment. I can only say how intensely vulnerable you feel in such circumstances. You are completely at the mercy of others. There is nothing you can do except wait. I prayed. In my abject weakness, I prayed for the strength to withstand any violence inflicted on me.

A long time elapsed, or at least it seemed to be a long time. I was just sitting there in limbo, waiting. Finally, there was the sound of approaching voices. My heart missed a few beats. This was it. There was no escape. Without a word, the guards pushed me back down the corridor and into my cell. To say I was relieved would be an understatement, but what was it all about? Was this treatment some kind of psychological way of breaking down my resistance? All the while, the shrieks and screams carried on in the distance. Why had I been excused from brutal treatment? What was going on? Had my friends been similarly excused? Were they even alive? I was the kind of person who liked to be in control, and getting answers to questions was one way of keeping control. Clearly, this was not going to happen. How long was I going to be kept in ignorance?

During the long hours of solitary confinement, time seemed to lose all meaning. Hours merged into one another, and there was a grave danger of becoming completely disorientated. There was the slight suggestion of night-time when even the small ray of light coming through the tiny window was extinguished and a deeper darkness became all-enveloping. I tried to keep in some kind of physical shape by doing press-ups, lunges, and plenty of stretching exercises. As for mental stimulation, my main occupation was to think of a word and then work out a cryptic crossword clue. Given my circumstances, one of the words that sprang to mind was *nightshade*. Eventually I came up with, 'What can be made with eight hands?' Spiritual comfort was found in my favourite psalm, number 46. The psalmist writes about turmoil, various kinds of disturbance, and warfare, but he begins with the words, 'God is our refuge and strength, a very present help in trouble' and ends with the words 'be still, and know that I am God!' Those words gave me a great deal of strength.

After a lengthy passage of time, another mug of indeterminate liquid was passed through a slit in the door, along with some food. To describe the substance on the tin plate as food would be to give it a thoroughly undeserved ascription. Was it very hard, dry bread or simply cardboard? In the semidarkness, it was difficult to resolve the puzzle. All I can say is that it was completely tasteless and nearly broke my teeth. How long can anyone survive on such a meagre diet?

Exactly the same procedure took place over the next few days—or was it weeks? There was the enforced sitting in silence, blindfolded and bound, followed sometime later by paltry rations. In between were periods of daydreaming, fitful sleep, and wild dreams. The flights of fancy were an escape from my predicament. I would dream of living in a beautiful country mansion, being waited on by an army of servants, eating sumptuous food, and being surrounded by loving family and friends. It goes without saying that Inge often figured in my reveries. How I longed to embrace and kiss her. How I pined for the fresh, bracing air of Snowdonia. The mind has wonderful ways of protecting itself by denying reality. I was also helped by meditating on the crucifixion of Christ. I found the cross to be a very powerful symbol not only of human suffering but somehow a promise of new life. This can only be described as a mystery which I was in no position to solve. The image of the cross proved to be a very potent symbol for me in my hours of need.

16

The Unexpected

There are different kinds of freedom. It has been asserted that one can be truly free even when restricted to a prison cell. I seemed to recall somebody once saying, 'Go to your cell, and your cell will teach you all you want to know.' However, all I was interested in was my physical freedom. Let me feel the wind in my hair and the smell of fresh air in my nostrils. To my complete astonishment, this happened sooner than expected.

I woke from my usual fitful sleep to discover the door of my cell open. Was I dreaming? Was this some kind of cruel trick on a poor, defenceless soul? I gingerly crept to the door and slowly opened it, fully expecting to be met with a punch in the face by a grinning guard. No such thing happened.

There wasn't a guard in sight. I stood there, rooted to the spot, transfixed and hardly daring to breath, let alone move. Then as if on a given signal, the prisoners from the other cells in the corridor began to emerge, albeit very hesitantly. Imagine my delight at seeing my three friends still alive, if somewhat unkempt, unwashed, and unshaven. Presumably they thought the same of me; I hadn't checked myself out in a mirror for a considerable length of time.

After hugs and handshakes, the four of us sat down and tried to assess our position.

'It's great to see the three of you again. Have you all survived in one piece?' I wanted to know.

'I'm fine,' said Barrett. 'All I did was sit there for an hour or two with a blindfold on.'

'Where have all the guards gone?' I asked.

'My guess is that either the Allies are progressing quicker than anticipated, or there is the threat of a major blitzkrieg,' replied Barrett.

'How long have we been incarcerated?' Spencer asked.

'I have no idea,' I said. 'But at least we all seem relatively healthy and in good spirits, so that is excellent news,'

'Far too long,' shouted Henry, 'I've had enough of all this talking. I am absolutely starving.'

This was the cue to search for some food that was worthy of the name. We discovered the kitchen, but there was little there to assuage our appetites except a few tins of beans and some stale bread. Anything was an improvement on our previous diet. We wolfed down all we could lay our hands on. We even found a few bottles of *apfelsaft*. Never had apple juice tasted so much like nectar from the gods.

After feeding ourselves as much as we could and having a good wash and shave, we looked around for a change of clothes. If we were to survive, we had to look reasonably civilised and not like barbarians from another planet. Finally, thanks again to fabled German efficiency, we found that our papers had been neatly filed away. We were all set to emerge into the world again not quite sure of what to do next. Some other prisoners had already made up their minds. They left their place of incarceration at the earliest opportunity like bullets out of a gun; presumably, they knew where they were going. We four didn't even know where we were, geographically speaking. We surmised we were not far from the Rhine, but that was only a very small clue—the Rhine was a very long river. Being English and therefore the enemy, we had no idea how we would be treated if we were discovered by any native Germans. We decided to not take any chances and to proceed with extreme caution.

As we crept slowly away from our place of imprisonment, we realised we had been confined in an ancient, medieval castle. The keep and battlements were plain for all to see. There was even a drawbridge and moat. After being locked away in a dark, dingy, smelly hole, there is nothing quite like the smell of freedom, the taste of fresh air, the feel of the breeze in one's air, and the sight of an open sky. As it happened, dusk was falling, so we were able to wander slowly into the outskirts of a small town without being seen. We walked alongside a railway line until we came close to a station where we could see the sign: Cochem.

'I know where we are now,' Barrett declared with a note of relief in his voice. 'Cochem is on the Moselle River, and that flows into the Rhine at Koblenz.'

'That's great,' muttered Henry sarcastically. 'But how is that going to help. We are still a long way from merry old England. What are we going to do now?'

'I think before we decide to do anything, we should hide in those nearby woods. Otherwise, someone is bound to see us and raise the alarm,' were Spencer's wise words.

We found a secluded place to hang out for a while, and our discussion continued.

'I think it would be possible to follow the course of the Moselle up through Luxembourg and on into France,' Barrett suggested.

'That may be so,' retorted Spencer, 'but if the German army is on retreat, we will soon by engulfed by hordes of enemy soldiers who would be under fire from Allied forces. I don't find that prospect very enticing.'

'This may seem very silly, but my suggestion would be to sail downstream into the Rhine,' Henry ventured.

'In other words,' I rejoined, 'we would be returned to our original plan.'

'We might stand a chance, but only if we travel by night,' Barrett affirmed.

This was finally agreed, and the decision was unanimous. By this time, darkness had set in, and we moved towards the river. It was difficult to believe, but we found ourselves in a field of carrots. We wasted no time in harvesting as many as we could carry. Happily, we came across an early milkman on his rounds. Without a sound, we relieved him of a few pints. We had food and drink, and now all we needed was a mode of transport.

By the time we had reached the river, the sun was beginning to rise. We felt it was far too risky to attempt to travel in broad daylight, so we looked around for somewhere to hide. We came across what seemed to be a deserted cottage that was about to fall down. There was nothing left of the windows, the roof had a hole in it, and the door leaned on its hinges. This was an ideal hiding place, somewhere to lie low until darkness fell. However, before that we had to deal with the effect of eating too many beans in the prison kitchen; stomach cramps were taking hold. Thankfully, there was a toilet outside in the garden, dilapidated though it was, and we took turns expelling the offending waste matter and felt considerably better afterwards. The comfort of a deep sleep overtook us, but we were disturbed by voices outside. Not daring to breathe, we cautiously peered over a window sill and discovered some children playing in the adjacent field. Somewhat relieved, we returned to the land of Nod.

Night approached, and after a meal of raw carrots and milk, we crept out along the riverbank in search of a suitable craft.

'Before we go any farther,' Barrett suddenly said, 'I want to make sure we are doing the right thing. We may stand a better chance if we all went our separate ways.'

'We've been together so far. I think we should stay together,' Spencer replied.

'I agree completely,' remarked Henry. 'In any case, Malcolm is the only one of us who can speak the native lingo, so we really need him to stay with us.'

'Yes,' agreed Spencer, 'he may be all the difference between capture and freedom.'

I mumbled something about my German not being very good at all, but I was shouted down. It was we decided to stick together. There were quite a few small craft, but any engine would make a noise, and a sail would be easily seen. We alighted upon quite a large rowing boat that also had a canopy. This was ideal. In order to create the maximum disruption and confusion, we loosed a few boats from their moorings before we quietly set off on our rowing boat. Our hope was that by the time all the boats had been recovered and the loss of one discovered, we would be a long way away. So began our voyage down the Moselle towards Koblenz.

17

Father Rhine

We were able to make good headway because we were flowing with the current. As the sun began to rise, we approached the outskirts of Koblenz. We quickly came to a halt beneath a deep swathe of weeping willows. We were exhausted, but so far, so good. No one had come racing down the river in search of us. We covered ourselves with the canopy and quickly slipped into a deep sleep, only to be rudely awakened by the sound of approaching aircraft. Bombs began to fall. This was an Allied air raid.

Without much discussion, we realised this was our chance to get through the city without detection. All eyes would be focussed on the skies or hidden in shelters. We had slept well, and night was fast approaching. We rowed as fast as we could into the city. As expected, the artillery fire was intense, as was the amount of bombs. We could only hope and pray that we would be spared. The confluence of Mother Moselle and Father Rhine takes place at a famous landmark, *Deutsches Eck*, or German Corner, where we guessed there would be a lot of defensive artillery.

We were not disappointed, but happily, all the hardware was pointing to the skies. No one seemed to be looking at the river. There were explosions all around and even in the river, but amazingly, we flowed through Koblenz and into the Rhine undetected. Was God on our side? Is God on anyone's side, except those who, in the words of the prophet Micah, 'do justice, love kindness, and walk humbly with God' (Micah 6:8)? This wasn't the time for a philosophical discussion on the nature of God's actions. We kept our heads down and continued to row. Long before dawn broke, we were exhausted. Weeks of a near starvation diet and very little exercise had left the four of us weakened. The hard physical effort was taking its toll; moreover, our limited rations were beginning to run out.

Before long, there was a unanimous decision to find a place to lie low in order to rest and recover. This was easier said than done because this part of the Rhine formed a gorge and was actually the narrowest part of the river; it was noted for shipping mishaps. We kept going through the darkness, passing without seeing the Lorelei rock. Barrett, the walking encyclopaedia, whispered to us the story of how a beautiful girl wanted to take her own life because her true love was unfaithful. The local bishop, fascinated by her loveliness and humility, took her to a convent. On the way to the convent, she stopped at the cliff to look back on the palace of her truelove. When she saw him riding away, in despair she threw herself into the turbulent waters below. So the story goes, and ever since, the rock has been a huge tourist attraction. But for the moment, there was no attraction whatsoever. On the opposite bank to the rock sat the town of St Goar, and shortly after that, the river widened considerably. We felt it safer to find a secure resting place.

What a beautiful river the Rhine is, flowing right through the heart of Germany like an artery; it's the longest river in Western Europe. No wonder the Germans have used it as a natural defence against all aggressors. At the end of World War I, the Rhineland was subject to the Treaty of Versailles. This decreed it would be occupied by the Allies until 1935, and after that it would be a demilitarised zone with the German army forbidden to enter. The Treaty of Versailles and this particular provision caused much resentment in Germany and is often cited as helping Hitler's rise to power. The Allies left the Rhineland in 1930, and the German army reoccupied it in 1936, which was enormously popular in Germany. Although the Allies could probably have prevented the reoccupation, Britain and France were not inclined to do so—a feature of their policy of appeasement to Hitler.

We eventually came across an old, decrepit boathouse which had obviously not seen a boat for many years. It lay at the end of a very long garden, so we assumed we could stay there for a day and not be disturbed. How wrong we were. The first signs of trouble were when a dog came sniffing around outside. This was quickly followed by a voice shouting, 'Fritz, komm hier.' The dog continued to sniff and then began to bark excitedly. There was nothing we could do. We had been discovered. We sat frozen to the spot. Slowly the old wooden door creaked open, and there stood a young teenage lad. He looked at us open-mouthed, in complete surprise. After what seemed like an age, without uttering a word, he turned and ran up the long garden towards the house. We waited. Rowing farther upstream in broad daylight was a certain recipe for disaster.

Eventually the lad returned with a lady, whom we presumed to be his mother.

'Was machen Sie hier?'

What were we doing there? I didn't know how to answer. On the spur of the moment, I decided to take a chance and tell her the truth.

'Do you speak English?'

'A little,' she replied.

'We are English and trying to get to the Swiss border,' I said.

We held our breath. Our future depended on this lady's reply.

'Machen Sie kein Angst. Ich werde Ihnen helfen.'

Sighs all round. She had told us not to worry, and she was going to help us. Could she be believed? Could we trust her?

She beckoned with her finger, and we meekly followed up the garden into the house. Were we literally being led up the garden path? The next incident helped to assuage our fears. As we sat in a fairly comfortable lounge, surrounded by well-laden bookshelves, the smell of soup drifted in from the kitchen. We sat there, silently taking in our surroundings. This was a well-furnished and well-kept house. Apart from all the bookshelves, there was a lovely display cabinet and sideboard which looked typically German. In front of the three-piece suite on which we were sitting was a long, low coffee table. We were startled out of our reverie as the lady and her son appeared with some steaming bowls of *kartoffeln suppe*. Never has potato soup tasted so delicious. We devoured it, hardly taking time to breathe. We had been so busy surviving that we hadn't realised just how hungry we were. Our repast was concluded with a small glass of beer. Were we in heaven?

The lady apologised for such a scanty meal. 'I am so sorry, but food is very short. We do not have much.'

With one voice, we uttered out heartfelt thanks.

'Can you tell me why you are here?'

I was again the spokesman and related to her, as simply as I could, that we had been captured and had unexpectedly been freed from our prison.

'I know why,' she said. 'The English forces are now in France, and German forces are, how do you say, coming back.'

'Retreating,' I said.

'Yes, retreating. Gott sei Dank, der Krieg ist fast beendet.'

This was the first news we'd heard for weeks.

'My husband is a soldier, and I know not if he is alive or dead.'

We all expressed out sadness and concern. She could see that we still had worried expressions on our faces.

'My husband is German, but I am from Holland. I do not support this war. That is why I will help you.'

'How can you possibly help us?' I asked her.

'You will not get to the border in that old boat of yours. Either it will sink, or you will be seen. My uncle is also Dutch and has a large barge on which he carries goods from the north down into Switzerland. I will try to get you on one of his journeys. For now, you must stay here in my cellar.'

She must have noticed our worried expressions.

'There is no problem,' she said. 'This house is on its own. There are no neighbours, and my son is on holiday from school.'

Our sighs of relief could have been heard a few miles away.

18

God Talk

The cellar was quite well furnished. There was a three-piece suite, albeit well worn, and even some bunk beds. Apparently, in happier times the extended family often came to stay. After taking stock of our bearings, we began to relax.

'There must be a God after all,' I said. 'He has looked after us so far and found us a comfortable place to rest and recover. It really is an answer to prayer.'

Quick as a flash, Henry retorted, 'What has it got to do with God? We are here purely by good fortune and nothing else.'

Barrett agreed. 'If God is looking after us, why is he not looking after all the innocent people who have been killed in this stupid war?'

I had to admit I found it a difficult question to answer, but Spencer came to my aid. 'We don't always know how God answers our prayers, but Christians believe he does, and that is a matter of faith.'

Henry stated his case in no uncertain terms. 'That is just being airy-fairy. I'm a scientist, and I only deal with facts. Give me the evidence.'

Barrett was less dogmatic. 'I'm not at all sure science has all the answers. I know for a fact that you have fallen in love a few times. What does science have to say about love?'

'Quite so,' agreed Spencer. 'Beauty is in the eye of the beholder, not the scientist.'

'You can say what you like, but at the end of the day, science has taught us many things about the world and the universe in which we live. Indeed, theologians have changed their minds many times because of the discoveries of science. How many people still believe the earth is flat, or that the earth is at the centre of the universe, or that God is sitting up there somewhere on big white cloud?'

'OK, you've made your point,' said Spencer with a big sigh. 'But what about this horrendous war we are in—or the Great War? Have scientists discovered an answer to how we may peacefully solve our problems and conflicts?'

This presented an opportunity for me to jump in. 'As the good book says, don't use evil to overcome evil. I would even go so far as to say that violence always begets violence. Is dropping bombs on innocent people really the best way for a civilised society to solve its problems?'

'Oh, we know about your pacifism. I suppose you'd be happy being overrun and ruled by the Germans. Don't we have a moral obligation to defend ourselves?' This was Barrett's viewpoint.

'I'd be more than happy to defend myself and others, but only by nonviolent means. If I didn't believe that, I wouldn't be here, I'd be back in Manchester reading my theology books. I believe in practical theology and putting my beliefs into practice, not keeping them locked up in a theology faculty—or for that matter, keeping them in church for use only on Sundays.'

Everybody fell silent for some time, but eventually Henry interrupted our thoughts.

'You still haven't answered my question about prayer. I know you say God always answers our prayers, but we don't always get the answer we want. That seems to me God can't lose. Heads, he wins; tails, I lose.'

Spencer rose to the bait.

'In one sense, you are right. Who can know the mind of God? I think the psalmist says something like God's thoughts are not like our thoughts, and neither are his ways like our ways. On the other hand, many Christians believe God has clearly answered their prayers.'

I joined in with a favourite quotation of my mother from Tennyson: 'More things are wrought by prayer than this world dreams of.'

Henry was not convinced. 'Where is the scientific evidence that God answers prayer?'

Again a silence descended. To be having this esoteric conversation at all, given our predicament, struck me as quite bizarre. Here we were on foreign soil, a long way from the white cliffs of Dover, with only a slim chance of reaching home. Yet we were arguing the toss about whether God answers prayer. I think psychologists call this a displacement activity.

I couldn't help wondering, *If there is no God, why are we here at all? What is life all about?* Out of the blue arose an irrational thought: *What if the Hokey Cokey is what life is all about?*

Our daydreaming was broken by the appearance of the lady of the house with some steaming cups of coffee. This was accompanied by a wonderful piece of homemade gateau. What luxury!

'I hope you like cake,' she said. 'I managed to find enough sugar and flour to put something together.'

'Do we like cake?' exclaimed Henry. 'Do monkeys like bananas?'

'Silly question,' murmured Spencer as he took a large slice from the plate that was place before him.

'You are being very kind to us,' said Barrett, 'but we don't even know your name.'

'My name is Anne,' the lady replied. 'My son's name is Hans.' Before any of us could reply, she went on. 'But I do not need to know your names.' She was clearly working on a need-to-know basis.

Fair enough, I thought. There was no doubt in my mind that Anne could be completely trusted. I was not so sure about Hans.

19

Alarm Bells

The days passed into a week with only our somewhat heated discussions to pass the time. Venturing out was far too risky and would endanger Anne's life as well as our own. We heard via the radio that the Allied forces were progressing well into France and pushing towards the German border. The newscaster expressed the view this was only a minor setback for the German forces, and they would soon be retaliating. Our view was this was a piece of German propaganda to keep the citizens hopeful. The news notwithstanding, we were beginning to get frustrated and bad-tempered with each other. Cabin fever was setting in yet again. The little mannerisms we each had became irritating, and simple, innocent comments developed into petty arguments.

'Why are you always picking your nails?' Henry once blurted out at me.

'Can't you think of a different tune to hum?' Barrett shouted at Spencer.

'It looks a really lovely day out there,' murmured Spencer.

'No, it's not', retorted Henry. 'It is an awful day, and I can't stand being with you lot much longer.'

In this manner, each day was punctuated by barbed comments like pieces of shrapnel piercing the air. We saw little of Anne and her son. One of them appeared from time to time to bring us some food and refreshment. However, on one occasion, much to our consternation, Hans brought a teenage girl friend with him.

'This is a friend of mine,' he explained, 'She wanted to meet you and practise her English.'

Barrett quickly replied as politely as he could, 'It is very nice to meet you, but talking to us will endanger your life. Please, don't tell anyone you have seen us.'

'This is very important,' Spencer agreed. 'Do not tell anyone.'

This was very naïve of Hans, and it increased our desire to leave as quickly as possible. We had no idea of know whether this friend would betray us and tell her parents (or anyone else) about our whereabouts. Moreover, we felt like animals in a zoo cage being stared at, having no choice and no escape.

When they left, Henry put forward a thought that was a bit disturbing. 'I'm not convinced that Hans brought his friend so she could improve her English. Maybe he wanted to show her that he hadn't been lying about the visitors in his cellar.'

'That is more than likely,' surmised Spencer. 'In which case, he could have told any number of people.'

The next time we saw Anne, we expressed our concern.

'We are very uneasy that your son visited us with one of his friends,' I said. 'Has he told anyone else?'

'You can trust him,' Anne replied. 'The girl you saw is a very good friend of Hans. They have known each other for a long time. I feel sure she can be trusted.'

'I'm not convinced,' said Henry.

'There is something else we are worried about,' added Barrett. 'We don't know when your husband is going to return from the front. If he has been injured, he could turn up at any moment.'

'I can't help you there,' replied Anne.' I have no way of knowing where my husband is. I have not received any letters of weeks. For all I know, he may be have been shot.'

'That would be very sad news for you,' Spencer said, 'but given our situation, I think we need to leave here as soon as possible.

There was little else to say. It was patently clear that our presence in Anne's house was becoming more hazardous by the minute.

Moreover, we were concerned that Anne's involvement with us could make her life very difficult if she was discovered.

As a result of these thoughts, the four of us decided to take our chances and move on in our little boat. Having persuaded Anne this was the best course of action for us and also in her best interest, she gave us as much food as she could possibly spare. In all honesty, there wasn't much, but one had to hand it to her. Anne had been a brick looking after us without giving a thought for her own safety. She had also given all she could spare from her larder. Such people make the world a better place to live in. I was reminded of the prayer of Ignatius: 'To give and not to count the cost, to fight and not to heed the wounds, to toil and not to ask for any reward save that of knowing we do God's will.'

As night fell, we pushed off, having offered our profuse and heartfelt thanks to Anne and Hans. My goodness, it was good to be back in the open air again after being cooped up for over a week. It was good to feel again fresh breeze on one's face. The experience was so bracing and enlivening, and our spirits were uplifted. The moon was merely a faint crescent, so we were enclosed in darkness. Not a word passed our lips; we knew the procedure. Rowing progressed with hardly a sound, just a gentle swish as the oars left the water and a little splash as they reentered. We made good progress for a few hours, and I was beginning to enjoy the stillness and get in touch with my inner self when suddenly a searchlight appeared in the distance, moving towards us. This was a vessel that was clearly searching for something or somebody. Had we been betrayed? Could Hans have given the game away?

We quickly sought refuge in some dense reeds by the river bank. We used what we could to camouflage the outline of the boat and then lay down flat out in the bowels of our craft. We heard the engine of the approaching vessel. It was travelling very slowly, clearly taking time to make a thorough search as the beam of light swung across the river from the left bank to right bank. Our hearts pounded, and sweat poured off us. Surely we would be discovered. We waited, hearts in mouth, for a German voice to say, 'Wer ist Da?' 'Who is there?'

Nothing happened. A voice did not shatter the silence with its violent demand. We had not been spotted. The vessel slowly moved past us. We lived to fight another day. Sighs of relief all round. The change in atmosphere was palpable, and we could have broken open a bottle of champagne and had a party. Of course, that was impossible. All we could do was stay there for a few hours to ensure the search party was not returning. We all visited the land of Nod and slept like logs.

We slowly awoke and stretched our stiffened limbs. The sun was shining, and we felt good to be alive. We ate some of the provisions that Anne had thoughtfully provided for us, and then we patiently awaited nightfall, observing a number of boats that chugged past us. We noticed that some of them carried a Dutch flag. Could we take Anne's advice and risk showing ourselves to one of them?

20

The Flying Dutchman

Clearly there was a lot at stake. If we hailed a Dutch vessel, we had everything to gain. On the other hand, if we fell into the wrong hands, we could lose everything. There was no way of identifying which vessels would be sympathetic and which would be antagonistic. The only visible sign was a Dutch flag. We took stock of our position. Realistically, we were all pretty exhausted with the rowing. Furthermore, our boat was beginning to show signs of wear and tear. In fact, it had become necessary to bail water out from time to time. How long could we continue in this way? The odds were stacked heavily against us. Good fortune had been our companion thus far, or maybe God was with us, but how long could we continue in this way? The Allies may well be winning the war, but we couldn't wait weeks in the hope they would eventually arrive. The decision was taken to hail the next Dutch barge that we saw.

We didn't have to wait very long. A sturdy-looking craft was gently ploughing its way down the river. We had ample time to come out of hiding and reveal ourselves. The boatman saw our white flag, immediately slowed down, and drifted towards us. Without asking for an explanation, he threw a rope towards us, and we quickly scrambled aboard. Barrett was the last one, and his final act was to hole the boat that had served us so well. The last thing we wanted was someone to find an unmanned rowing boat. We watched with mixed feelings as it quickly sank out of sight.

It was then time to meet our rescuer. Could this be Anne's uncle? That would be stretching the laws of probability a step too far.

We soon discovered the man steering the vessel was called Vincent. He had no hesitation in telling us his name. We also ascertained that he was not Anne's uncle. Vincent was a big, jovial bear of a man with a huge beard, ruddy complexion, a cap at a rakish angle, and a pipe hanging from his mouth. He was a prime example of all one could imagine a sailor to be like. Vincent and his young son were the only crew on the boat. My gut instinct told me we had landed in friendly hands. We related to him the bare bones of our story. He wasn't really interested. As soon as he knew we were English, that was sufficient. He laughed loudly and said he was more than happy to help.

'I'm fed up with this cursed war,' he said. His words were peppered with what I assumed were Dutch expletives. 'Life in Holland has been unbearable. I am only allowed to leave the country because they need my coal in the south. Sometimes I have to travel with a German soldier, but not now. They have all been called away to the front.'

This was all very good news, not to mention that his English was excellent. But did he have any ideas to avoid us being seen?

'No problem,' he said. 'You can be my crew.'

And so it was that we dressed ourselves to look like working seamen. Vincent had some spare overalls and caps, and before long, with some dirt rubbed into our hands to give them a gnarled appearance, we looked the part. Onwards we sailed upstream. We began to move faster, and we had time to admire the view. The hillsides were covered in vineyards. We were well into the season of autumn—as the poet Keats wrote, 'a season of mists and mellow fruitfulness'. The vines were laden with delicious-looking grapes. I had been brought up in a household that was strictly teetotal; my parents had signed the so-called pledge. My attitude was all things in moderation, including alcohol. Indeed, at that point in time I felt a good glass of wine would be perfectly acceptable, accompanied by a morsel of tasty cheese. No such luck. There was no time for daydreaming—concentration was the order of the day. Who knew what lay round the next bend in the river?

Happily, we had no concerns about Vincent. It was obvious we were in good hands. I think he could have found his way down the Rhine with his eyes shut. He had been travelling up and down the river all his life. Hardly without noticing, we had sailed through Mainz and Wiesbaden and were well on the way to Ludwigshafen. There was no way we could sail through the night; Vincent told us in no uncertain terms that this would be very dangerous. In fact, the Germans had prohibited any traffic on the Rhine during the hours of darkness. There was nothing for it other than to moor at Ludwigshafen. As we approached the city, it was plain for all to see Allied bombers had done their worst.

'What on earth has happened here?' Henry blurted out.

'It looks as though a few bombs have been dropped on it,' Spencer said drily.

'That is precisely what has happened,' explained Vincent. 'Ludwigshafen is an industrial city, so it was an important target for the Allies. The same is true of Mannheim, on the opposite bank. Both cities have been almost destroyed for the same reason: they are dependent on heavy industry.

'As a matter of interest,' he added, 'you may also like to know that a large number of Jews from both cities have been deported, but I have no idea what has happened to them.'

I have no idea how he came to know this piece of information, but it stimulated in me a train of thought. I knew Matthew's gospel invited the view that the Jews were responsible for the death of Jesus, but was that any reason for continued anti-Semitism? Could a case really be made for collective Jewish guilt? Surely other people were also involved in the crucifixion of Jesus. In any case, didn't Jesus say, 'Forgive them, for they know not what they do'? Did people have to keep on hating Jews? Where did forgiveness come in, if indeed they were guilty in the first place?

These thoughts rambled through my head as we gently came to a quiet mooring a little way from the city centre and surrounded by many other barges. In this way, we hoped to n to arouse any suspicion.

Little did we know at the time that the city's defences were totally preoccupied with the rapidly advancing Allies. For safety's sake, and because we were so close to other boats, the four of us decided to remain in a cabin below the deck. From somewhere, Vincent conjured up some potatoes, carrots, and beer; there was no meat because rationing had become very strict in Germany.

As soon as the sun broke through, we pulled up anchor and quietly slipped away. We had been completely untroubled during the night. Vincent wasted no time in getting underway. He said he wanted to get us beyond Karlsruhe by nightfall. At this point, the Rhine ran alongside the Black Forest, and Vincent's plan was to disembark us between Karlsruhe and Basle so we could trek the short distance through the forest over the border and into Switzerland and Lake Constance. His view was that it was far too dangerous to attempt to cross the border in his boat. Furthermore, he had to unload his cargo at Basle and therefore travelling farther south would simply court unnecessary suspicion.

Vincent took the barge as near to the bank as he could, and the long-legged Barrett was the first to jump for the bank. He sprang across with a rope so the three of us could hang on to that if we should fall into the river. We all made it without mishap, or just about. Of course, before disembarking, we said our heartfelt thanks to Vincent and wished him well for the rest of his journey.

21

The Black Forest

The Black Forest is a largely wooded mountain range rising to a height of nearly five thousand feet. For all we knew, we could be in the middle of the New Forest in England. We were in the middle of nowhere. We followed the sun and headed south towards the highest point, which Barrett informed us was called Feldberg. There was no point in walking through the night. The forest lived up to its name and was completely black. We could easily have gone round in circles. We were fortunate enough, after a couple of hours walking, to find a well-worn trail. We followed this but didn't stay together. For safety's sake, we stayed well apart and certainly kept an ear open for the sound of voices or whatever.

The forest was a clear reminder of days spent weeks earlier in Königsforst, near Kleineichen. I wondered about the family I had spent time with, especially Inge. What was happening to her? To my surprise, I seemed to have intense feelings for her. I found myself worrying about her and wondering if we would ever meet up again. My daydreaming was interrupted by the sound of a twig breaking. We all stopped dead in our tracks and crouched low to the ground. Then to our surprise and relief, a couple of deer wandered onto our path. They were as surprised as we were, and as soon as they saw us, they scampered away. The thought of a tasty piece of venison fleetingly crossed my mind.

Henry said as much. 'That would make a tasty bit of dinner,' he ventured, licking his lips.

The rest of us told him to be quiet. You never know who could be in the forest and wonder what the noise was about. In the distance, we heard the sound of bells. These were not church bells but those worn by cattle in those parts. We could only guess we were coming near to some grazing land and possibly a farmhouse. We proceeded with caution. On coming to the edge of a field on the slopes of the Feldberg, we saw a young girl rounding up the cattle for milking. Before we could duck back into the woods, she spotted us. What could we do? A dilemma if ever there was one.

We could pretend to be hikers out for the day, but we were hardly dressed for it. In any case, why weren't four fit young men at the front and fighting for the country? Maybe we were foresters who had lost their way. An unlikely tale if ever there was one. Perhaps we were foreigner soldiers who had escaped and were on their way to the Swiss border.

'What a beauty she is,' murmured Henry under his breath.

As always, we could rely on Henry to blurt out what was on everyone's mind. Beauty or not, she didn't seem in the least bit perturbed by our sudden appearance, perhaps because she had a rather large sheep dog in attendance. Maybe her father was, at that moment, pointing a rifle in our direction. We didn't wait to find out. Quite simply, we legged it up the Feldberg. This is where all our arduous training in Snowdonia paid dividends. If there was to be a hue and cry our pursuers were going to have to move very quickly to catch us.

We reached the summit in what seemed like no time at all but in reality was probably about two hours. While gazing at the distant horizon, we saw the snow-capped Alps, and in the middle distance were the glimmering waters of Lake Constance, our destination. The lake formed the border between Germany and Switzerland. We looked behind us.

'Nobody is chasing after us,' I said with relief.

'I'm not at all surprised,' Spencer replied laconically. 'Why bother chasing us when all they've got to do is ring up the border guards and tell them to expect our arrival?'

His logic couldn't be faulted. I had expressed relief far too soon. We still had a long way to go, so we pressed on, only briefly admiring the view. The top of the mountain presented no cover, and we could imagine distance binoculars trained on our every movement.

As soon as we reached some forest, Barrett stopped in his tracks. 'We need a plan. Otherwise, we shall end up in the arms of the border guards. Has anyone any ideas?'

There was complete and utter silence. Not a word was spoken for quite some time.

True to form, Henry broke the ice. 'I think we should just go for it in the hope that the guards haven't been warned. We will get through somehow.'

Barrett was inclined to agree. 'Lake Constance is huge. There won't be guards along the whole of the bank. Incidentally, the bank of the lake is actually the border. Once we are in the lake, we will be in Switzerland. The lake is much narrower towards the east. It may be possible we could swim to one of the many islands.'

Spencer joined in. 'I don't share your optimism. In any case, I think we stand a better chance if we split up and meet again on the other side.'

I confessed to having nothing to add to the discussion.

Silence again descended.

'I know,' said Spencer. 'Let's find somewhere to rest up for a few days and give time for the alarm to die down.'

'That seems entirely reasonable to me,' I ventured.

'That sounds good to me,' agreed Barrett. 'This is walking country, so there is bound to be a rambler's hut somewhere nearby. Keep your eyes peeled.'

We set off once again, feeling more confident now we had a plan. Within a short space of time, a small wooden hut came into view. Happily, there was no one inside, but there were some tins of food someone had thoughtfully provided for hikers, and we found them very satisfying.

Henry suddenly blurted out, 'We can't possibly stay here. This is one of the first places any search party will look for. It is so obvious. We must find somewhere less obvious.'

Spencer nodded his head in agreement. 'Henry, for once I am in total agreement with you. The sooner we get out of here, the better.'

'Hang on a minute,' Barrett exclaimed. 'No one is going to come up here at this time of day. It will soon be pitch-black outside. At least let's spend the night here in relative comfort and move out at first light.'

No one could argue with that. A good night's sleep was precisely what the doctor ordered.

22

The Cave

We left our refuge as dawn was breaking, ensuring that there were no visible traces of our visit. We took some of the tins of food with us. I think hikers were supposed to leave some money as payment, but that was obviously beyond us; none of us had any cash. I felt quite guilty about this, but it was a case of needs must. There was no way of knowing where we would find food again.

The noise of running water attracted our attention. Soon we came across a waterfall pouring down the mountain side. The water had worn the cliffs smooth, and they were glistening in the sunlight. On closer inspection, there appeared to be a large opening behind the cascading water. To our delight, we discovered a large cave. The noise was far too great for any conversation, but with one accord we clambered round the back of the fall and entered the cave.

Ever resourceful, Barrett actually had a torch with him; I think he had procured it from the barge a couple of days earlier. With the benefit of this small light, we progressed deeper and deeper into the cave. Here, we could hide out for as long as we deemed it necessary. No one could possibly find us. Fresh water was obviously not a problem. There was an unlimited supply, and we had the purloined provisions from the cabin. When conversation became possible again, we decided to take it in turns to stay on watch at the mouth of the cave whilst the others remained in darkness farther inside. The torch battery had to be preserved for as long as possible.

It was just as well we had kept someone on guard because later in the day, people and dogs could be made out through the gushing water. Spencer was on guard, and he came back to tell us we had visitors. We moved farther into the cave and stumbled upon a small stream tumbling downwards. We carefully picked our way along the stream and moved ever deeper into the bowels of the cave. In this way, if our visitors ever ventured this far into the cave, we conjectured that any scent would be lost in the stream. We were not wrong. People or dogs did not come anywhere near us.

I have to say that we spent a very uncomfortable night in the cave. There was no way of getting a restful night. Was it night, or was it daytime? There was no way of knowing. We were enveloped in a solid wall of blackness, and dampness hung in the air so heavily that it seemed to enter our bones. The only advantage presented by the darkness was that it allowed us privacy when going to the toilet. Conversation was sparse.

'How I long for a lovely comfortable bed.'
'I would love a very hot shower with lots of soap.'
'I could do with someone to massage my aching limbs.'
'Wouldn't it be good to have some female company?'
'Not in these surroundings.'
'I wonder what is happening to the Allies. Are we winning the war?'
'Will we ever get back home?'
'Whose silly idea was it to escape into Switzerland?'
'Wasn't that cowgirl a real beauty?'
'I'm longing to see my girlfriend again. She doesn't even know whether I'm still alive.'
'I wonder where this stream comes out. Perhaps we should follow it.'

Comments like these punctuated the night, making it more bearable, but the last two sentences hung in the air with a kind of expectancy.

23

The Descent

Following the stream was perilous. At any moment, we could be hit by a falling stone, or we could slip and fall who knew how far. Obviously, we were not roped together. This was indeed a dangerous descent. We kept on going down and down. Sometimes the descent was very steep, but at other times it was gentler.

I have to confess this whole experience was way outside my comfort zone. My preference without a doubt is the open air. I need to feel the wind on my face and see an expanse of the sky about me. Here, in this situation, I began to have strong feelings of claustrophobia. As a distraction, my mind turned to the plight of the early Christians living in the catacombs in Rome. How did they survive? Was there an endless supply of candles? How did they cook any food? Was it possible to light a fire? Did they enjoy any home comforts at all? Was it damp and cold all the time? They must have had an incredible faith to endure such privations. Indeed, the story of the rise of the early Christian Church against the power of the Roman Empire is quite remarkable and testimony to the faith and witness of the first Christians.

'Watch out,' cried Barrett, who was leading the way and switching on his torch from time to time. 'The stream seems to be going through a kind of tunnel.'

There was nothing for it but to crawl along on all fours. Some people enjoy exploring caves. I am not one of them. The experience was getting worse by the minute. The darkness was closing in around me. I repeatedly scratched myself on protruding rock, and the cold water was beginning to seep through my clothes. There was a damp, clammy smell in the air. This was not my idea of fun. I simply gritted my teeth and followed, touching Barrett's foot occasionally to ensure he was still there. In like manner, Henry, who was following me, touched my feet.

Our progress along this section was very slow. I'm not at all sure how Barrett managed to keep moving. He must have banged his head a number of times, but he still retained his consciousness. Eventually, we were able to stand again, but to our horror, a quick flash of the torch revealed that the stream had disappeared over the edge of what seemed to be a precipice. There was no way we could turn back. We had to keep moving forward, onwards and downwards.

This time our climbing was painfully slow. We took each step with great care and precision. Having come this far, there was no way we were going to do something silly and fall to certain death. In particular, Henry, who was bringing up the rear, didn't want to send a loose stone careering down to hit one of us on the head. Extreme caution was the order of the day. If ever there was a good bonding exercise, this was it. All the time, we took extreme care to look after each other, carefully holding each other's feet until they had reached a firm base. For one of us to incur a serious injury would have been disastrous, especially having almost attained our goal. After what seemed like a lifetime of inching our way downwards an almost vertical cliff face, we reached level ground. In sheer relief, we fell exhausted to the floor.

'That was one heck of a climb,' Spencer pronounced, verbalising something we knew all too well.

'I vote we stay here a while,' I said. 'We need to catch our breath and recover some strength.'

The suggestion seemed to go down quite well, or at least no one had the energy to disagree. The good news was we still had some food left from the cabin, and we quickly devoured the remains. Fortunately, Barrett had his Swiss army knife with him, and he used it as a tin opener.

After having eaten, rested, and relaxed, we felt able to proceed. This time the going was much easier. The ground was beginning to flatten out, and before long we saw a small pinprick of light in the distance. We slowly and cautiously moved to the opening, and there before us, in all its glory, was Lake Constance. What an amazing stroke of luck. The stream continued over about a hundred yards of gravel and fed into the lake. There was a small problem: the gravel path was very exposed, but on the edge of the water, marking the border, a vicious tangle of barbed wire blocked our way.

Within minutes, a border guard appeared and patrolled along the fence line. Thankfully, we were well hidden as we surveyed the scene. That was the good news. The bad news was we were stuck.

24

Lake Constance

What a pity nobody had thought to bring wire cutters or thick gloves! We seemed to have reached a dead end. How could we find a way out of our dilemma? Conversation was even quite difficult because we didn't want to be detected. We retreated back from where we had come so that we could speak to each other and devise a strategy. However, before doing so, we ensured that the patrols continued even during the hours of darkness. They did, with the addition of searchlights coming from a distant gantry. Fortune had well and truly deserted us.

Spencer began our deliberations by saying, 'I think we need some kind of diversion to take the guard away from the wire.'

'I know: let's all run naked along the beach.'

Barrett's annoyance at this stupid remark from Henry was palpable. 'That is not at all helpful. Try to be serious, just for once.'

I added my two pennies' worth. 'If we could overpower the guard, maybe I could quickly put on his uniform and continue his patrol.'

'Yes, but how are we going to get anywhere near him without being seen?' The logic and common sense of Spencer was difficult to refute.

'I suggest we all sleep on this and hope we have some inspiration in the morning.' Nobody argued against Barrett's suggestion, so that was that for the time being.

I can't say any of us slept well, but we benefitted from some much-needed rest.

Henry was the first to wake. 'I know,' he said. 'Why don't I pretend to be a down and out vagrant?'

In all honesty, that did not require much of an imagination. His clothes were torn. His hair was dishevelled. He hadn't washed or shaved for a couple of days. If anyone looked the part, Henry did.

'What then?' I enquired.

'Well, if I can get the guard to turn his back, whilst he is questioning me, Barrett can creep up on him and knock him out with a rock between his shoulders.'

'I think the word you are looking for is dry-gulch,' Spencer interjected.

Silence fell. Was this plan workable, or was it too outrageous?

Eventually Spencer said the obvious. 'We have no other plan.'

We decided to put the plan into action because dusk was falling and it was just before the searchlights were switched on. There was a slight probability that anyone watching could be deceived by the shadows of the fading light.

I ventured to ask one more thing. 'How do we get through the barbed wire?'

'Simple,' said Henry. 'When I put on the guard's clothes, you can use mine to wrap round your hands and force the wire apart to make a pathway through.'

'There is a minor detail,' muttered Spencer very deliberately. 'Who is going to volunteer to knock the guard on the head?'

'Me,' said Barrett without a moment's hesitation.

I breathed a quiet sigh of relief. Hitting somebody with a view to knocking them out was simply not in my repertoire. Moreover, I couldn't help thinking—although I didn't say anything—that this all sounded far too easy for words. But the plot had been hatched, and we needed to put it into practice. As the afternoon wore on, tension began to mount. Would this plan succeed, or was it far too audacious?

In the twilight, Henry stumbled out into the shadows towards the direction of the oncoming guard.

'Halt!' A voice full of authority rang out, and a gun was pointed in the direction of Henry.

Henry's hands immediately shot up into the air, carrying a white and very dirty handkerchief. The guard approached very cautiously and full of suspicion. Somehow, Henry succeeded in shuffling round so that his back was to the lake; the guard therefore had his back to us. I have never seen Barrett move so fast. With his long, loping strides, he came upon the guard in no time and struck him mightily hard between the shoulders. The guard fell like a stone. Like lightning, we stripped the guard, and I put on his uniform. I'm not sure this was entirely necessary, but it did give the other three precious time to find a way through the wire because if anyone was looking on, they would still see a guard. Our plan went like clockwork. In semidarkness and just as the searchlight came on, I crawled through the wire and joined the others in the lake.

We swam as hard as we could until we were out of range of any stray bullets, and then we headed for the nearest island. An hour of hard swimming brought us to dry land, and there we were met by the sole inhabitant. He greeted us with a smile, and we knew we were in safe hands. Not only that, but we had escaped from Germany. The man clearly knew we were on the run, and without a word he put us in his motorboat and took us to the other side of the lake. This was a good distance away and was far too far for us to have swum.

Everything went smoothly from there. With a little help from some of the locals, who were only too glad to lend assistance, we found our way to the nearest airport and managed to hitch a lift on a transport plane to dear old Blighty.

25

Endings and a Beginning

The plane landed, and we came to the parting of our ways. This was not easy. I have to confess there was a large lump in my throat. I know we were grown men, and we were not expected to reveal our emotions. We were supposed to keep the traditional stiff upper lip, but we had been through so much together, and now we were separating and going off to our different lives. The war was coming to a conclusion, so we were about to pick up our lives where we left them. There were lots of hugs and handshakes, even some tears, but our farewells were made somewhat easier by the promise to have an annual reunion.

'See you all next year,' Henry shouted, trying to be cheerful.

'Yes, I hope we can all make it,' Barrett replied.

'Maybe you will get yourself hitched,' Spencer said to me.

'Not me,' I said. 'I'm quite happy to stay as I am. Anyway, I've got a lot of studying to catch up with. You get back to your girlfriend—and don't forget to invite us to your wedding. You as well, Henry, and give her a kiss from me.'

'No chance,' he shouted as he disappeared into the distance.

And so with such familiar and friendly banter, we parted and went our separate ways. I made my way back to Manchester, to my parents' house, and recommenced my theological studies in the Faculty of Divinity. Once again I lived a more or less normal life, but it took a few weeks of adjustment. Who would believe what I had been through? With the money acquired from my active service, I was able to purchase an old Ford car for the princely sum of fifty pounds. This made my daily commute into the university much easier and less time-consuming.

In the following five or six years, I was eventually accepted into the ministry of the Methodist church. My three bosom pals all found themselves partners, and so I attended, as we all did, three weddings—and great occasions they were. They were times of great rejoicing, and of course a little time was spent in reminiscing. Needless to say, I was still single, but my car was proving to be very faithful until one day a friend happened to say there was a suspicious noise coming from the engine. Consequently, he came round and took out the engine. There it sat on the garage floor.

As I wondered if we would ever get the car back together again, the phone rang. I picked up the receiver and heard a lady's voice.

'Hello, Malcolm. I hope you are well. I am actually your friend Spencer's mother. Would you be interested in attending an international week of young people, which is starting in a few days' time? I would like to invite you.'

I was stunned by this totally unexpected invitation. In a few days, she said. Could I be ready by the weekend? This was all a bit too sudden for me. I liked to have things planned out and was not particularly keen on surprises, so I played for time. 'My car is in bits on the garage floor,' I stuttered. 'Anyway, where is it, and will I know anybody?'

'The week is taking place in a Christian Holiday Home in Penmaenmawr, North Wales, and there are young people attending from various countries in Europe. We are trying to develop positive relationships after all the destruction of the last war.'

My ears pricked up. I was all agog to hear the event would take place in the Penmaenmawr. 'What's the name of the Holiday Home?' I asked.

'Bryn' she said. 'It was requisitioned by the army during the war, but it has now been handed back to the former owners.'

I was speechless. Here was a wonderful opportunity to visit the place of my training—a place of many memories, some of them very painful. Without further ado and not having a clue about my transport, I agreed to attend.

'By the way, will anyone be there from Germany?' I asked, trying to sound nonchalant.

'Oh, yes. There is a young lady coming from Cologne. I think she is called Inge.'

I was overcome with emotion. Not only was I returning to Bryn, but also Inge was going to be there! One couldn't make it up. Fantastic.

Saturday found me on the road to North Wales. We had worked very hard to repair my car, or at least my friend had. He knew what he was doing; I had no idea and simply followed his instructions. My excitement mounted as I approached my old hunting ground. I wondered what Inge would look like and what reception she would give to me. I had hardly stepped out of the car when I saw Inge. She looked absolutely stunning and had grown into a beautiful young lady. I need not have worried about the kind of reception I would get. Without standing on any ceremony, she ran to meet me and warmly embraced me. I was overcome with emotion and just managed to hold back my tears of joy.

'Where have you been?' she exclaimed.

In my simplicity, I stated the obvious. 'I've been on the way in my little car.'

Then the penny dropped. She was really asking an existential question, not a matter of fact. Where had I been for so many long years? A detailed explanation of my studies was not appropriate at that point, so we gave each other a long, lingering hug.

On entering the house, I immediately noticed a framed set of words.

'Mankind is one great brotherhood, indivisible alike by religion, nationality, or colour, with God being the father of all. Our aim is to try to destroy those things which separate people from each other, to do away with the occasion of wars, and to put in their place some kind of loving fellowship.'

These were exactly the words that Inge's Dad had spoken to me.

'I know what you are thinking,' Inge said. 'All my family are well, although life was very hard immediately after the war. There was very little food for many months; everything was rationed. Papa was released from prison as soon as the war was over. He didn't suffer too much at the hands of the Gestapo.'

This was all music to my ears. As Inge talked, I couldn't help noticing again that she had matured into a rather beautiful young lady. She certainly could not be mistaken for a boy now—all her curves were in exactly the right places. I was delighted to see her again. No, I was ecstatic.

In the evening, we went for a romantic stroll in the moonlight along the promenade. I brought to mind the last time we had been for a walk together. Then, the situation had been fraught with danger, and we'd been surrounded by the dreadful, destructive chaos that war produced. Now, we were in a completely different place, both physically and emotionally. Of course, we hugged and kissed … and kissed … and kissed. The rest is history.

Lightning Source UK Ltd.
Milton Keynes UK
UKHW042310060919
349299UK00001B/20/P